ANGELS IN THE SNOW

Henrietta F. Ford

Second Edition

2010

Copyright 1999 by Henrietta F. Ford

Dedication

To all the victims of ALS, especially to my father,

Lester Shipley Ford, Jr.

Acknowledgements

I would like to thank my husband for his patience and encouragement. Thanks, Jim! You were right. One can pen mystery and suspense set in the peaceful countryside of Franklin County, Tennessee.

I would also like to thank Isbel Anders. I learned so much from her as she shared her experiences as an author, and her friendship gave me the confidence to persevere.

CHAPTER 1

Tuesday Night

He was cold and shivering. He couldn't stop shaking. He knew this place. He'd been here before. He looked down the uncarpeted stairs into the great room, recognizing the burgundy sectional sofa with loose black pillows. The longest section of the sofa was placed in front of a stone fireplace. The shorter sections curved to stand before a wide, sliding glass door.

He recognized the dog, too. It was a small white poodle, perfectly clipped into that ridiculous style that made it look like a deformed ballerina. The dog kept jumping up and down, hitting the glass door. Its mouth opened, shut, opened, shut. Small circles of crystallized condensation formed, marking the places where the dog's breath froze on the glass. But there was no sound.

The watcher looked beyond the glass door onto a familiar deck that was now being covered by the rapidly falling snow and sleet. Trees beyond the deck were beginning to sport a winter garb. Snow-covered branches waved wildly as if trying to disrobe the icy shroud. Tall tree trunks stood as if sketched in charcoal against the gray and white winter skyline. He watched as the storm worsened, nearly obstructing the view of the distant lake.

Suddenly the object of the poodle's frenzy came into his view. He knew her, also. Her tall, slim figure trod cautiously as her heavy boots slipped precariously on the frozen snow and ice. She wore no hood. Her blue denim jacket and her dark hair were sprinkled with ice pellets and snowflakes. Her hand moved to brush away a flake that had been trapped by her long, dark eyelashes. Squinting, her mocha-colored eyes targeted her destination.

At the end of the yard, just before the woods began, there stood a tall pile of logs, cut to fit exactly into the stone fireplace. The logs were heaped between two pine trees, which stood about eight feet apart. The abundance of logs seemed to predict a harsh winter. How many cords of wood had it taken to make a stack of logs so high? As if in slow motion, the girl trudged across the virgin snow toward the woodpile. Her gloved hand held the oak handle of a leather log carrier. Finally, she reached the woodpile.

He watched the familiar girl as she set the leather carrier on the ground and brushed snow from her jacket and jeans. Logs from last year's stock were scattered on the ground beside the high woodpile. Her strong hands retrieved logs from beneath the snow, shook them, and placed them in the leather carrier. He watched her work slowly.

The wind whipped the branches of a nearby stand of small dogwood trees. At the assault of the silent wind, the leafless arms of the trees undulated wildly, often tangled together, torn apart, and then whipped to the ground.

He was fascinated by the silent animation of the fragile limbs...long, dark, curved, moving. Then one tree appeared to move away from the others, taking on a human form. The figure moved into the clearing. The arms of the form were bent upward and held a large jagged rock above the head of the stooping girl. Suddenly, the rock was slammed downward. A second blow quickly followed, bashing the top of her skull. The impact of the blows flipped the girl onto her back, and her limp body seemed to float slowly, slowly onto the snow. Her arms and legs stretched outward as a child posed to play angels in the snow.

Only her chocolate eyes moved...first unfocused, then blinking against the snow, fixing upon the figure lurking above her. The jagged rock was again raised perilously, and then abruptly dropped to the ground. A dark sticky stain spread from the rock onto the snow, defiling the pure whiteness of the winter sheet with a hideous red stain.

The dog stopped jumping. It stood still and stiff. Its eyes fixed upon the girl already being covered with snow. Now, it began to shake...first slightly, now convulsively. Finally, the ridiculous-looking animal dropped to the floor and laid its pointed nose upon its paws.

The watcher continued to shiver. His mouth was dry, and his teeth chattered. The cold became unbearable as his neck and shoulders stiffened.

An excruciating, glaring light penetrated the tissue of his eyelids. He realized that wakefulness was his only escape from this misery. Ignoring the protests of his smarting muscles, he lifted himself onto his elbow and looked down upon the floor where lay the cause of all his anguish.

A blue down comforter that he had bought in Germany lay heaped upon the floor. Two large cats were curled up in its mounds of softness, while only a sheet covered his body.

"Get offa' that, you," he growled. "I'm freezing my tail off."

The orange mass of fur flattened his ears to his head and glared up at the source of this disturbance. The black pile of fur lay perfectly still.

He jumped out of bed and found a woolen robe and a pair of pile-lined moccasins in the closet. He realized that although he was still shivering, he was sweating profusely. Since the room was so bright, he thought that he must have overslept. As he turned from the closet, he saw that the woods outside his window had been transformed into a display of winter brilliance. Once naked trees were now blanketed in white. On the ground, fallen leaves and underbrush were carpeted with several inches of snow and crusty ice. A confused red cardinal tried in vain to peck seeds, now frozen to a plastic bird feeder. The driveway was completely hidden from view, as was his small pile of fireplace logs.

Now reality set in. He understood the significance of the dream: snow, cold, a dream about fetching logs for a fireplace, remembering he hadn't ordered enough logs this winter. Relieved, he bent down and snatched up the comforter, dumping the two fat cats onto the floor. He let out a loud sigh of relief.

CHAPTER 2

Wednesday Morning

Matthew Murray's youthful appearance gave no hint that he was a forty-five year old widower and father of two college-aged sons. His 6`2" frame supported well his taunt, fit body. His eyes were a clear dark green, and he wore his thick black hair short in order to control its natural curl.

Matthew worked as an independent consultant in the aerospace field. He had not always worked alone from the office in his home. For eighteen years, he was employed at the Arnold Engineering Development Center at Arnold Air Force Base, Tennessee. When his mother was diagnosed with dreaded Alzheimer's disease, Matt was determined to take care of her. It was then that his home became his workplace, and Matt became independent consultant/caretaker. His days and nights were indistinguishable as he struggled to fulfill the responsibilities to his mother and his career. His former associates at the Center questioned the wisdom of Matt's decision, but this work arrangement made it possible for him to take care of his mother.

After all, she had not hesitated to come all the way from Tidewater, Virginia that hot July day when he called to tell her that Jill had died, and he and his twin sons needed her very much. She'd stayed on with them through the years of childhood diseases, school plays, parent-teacher conferences, homework, football games and puberty. She also stood with Matt outside the college dormitory as the pair of perfectly matched young adults awkwardly attempted their manly good byes.

So when his mother's mere forgetfulness developed into anxiety and inexplicable behavior, Matt took her for a physical examination. Dr. Herold had explained that although an autopsy was the only way to accurately determine Alzheimer's disease, her symptoms and behavior were unquestionably characteristic of the disease.

Matt wrote a letter to his brother, reporting the doctor's opinion, and describing his career move that would enable him to be his mother's caretaker. Upon receipt of the letter, Steve called from Portsmouth, Virginia to question Matt's judgment.

"Got your letter about Mom," Steve said. "God, how awful! I can't believe it. Are the doctor's sure?"

"They are as sure of the diagnosis as they can be with Alzheimer's disease," Matt replied. "And even if they could diagnose beyond a doubt, there is no promising treatment."

Steve listened, and when Matt finished speaking, there was a long pause. "I'm worried about you, too, Matt. Have you really thought about what you're doing?"

"I've thought about it, Steve."

"Look guy, I know Mom has done a lot for you after Jill died, helping raise the twins and all, but you know that if Mom could think clearly, she'd be the first to discourage this."

"Yeah, but she can't think clearly."

"I know, I know. Listen, little brother, you got a good job. You'll need money to send Chad and Garth to college. We'll need money to take care of Mom. How do you know this consulting will work out?"

"I just know," Matt replied.

Steve tried another tact. "Say, you're not trying to make me feel guilty are you? I want to help, too. Let's just get together and talk about a way that, you know, won't totally change anyone's life."

"Wait, Steve, I'm not doing this to make anybody feel guilty. It's just something I want to do. Don't worry about me. I've really thought through this. It's gonna be all right...really."

Steve paused. "Okay, guy. Let me know if I can help. I love her, too, Matt. You know?"

"Yeah, I know."

"And I love you, too," Steve added. "Good-bye, Little Brother."

"Bye, Steve."

God, how he missed Steve! He missed sailing up to the Chesapeake Bay or down to the Outer Banks into the sounds with the sun and the wind. In Tidewater, there was always a breeze in summer, not like in Middle Tennessee, where Julys were hot and dry and still, like when Jill died.

For two years, Matt's mother roamed the house, opening drawers, searching closets, turning on water faucets, and hiding stores of irrelevant objects in shoe boxes and under mattresses. She called the home care nurses, who came to bathe her twice a week, by the names of long-dead relatives. Soon, she didn't recognize her son.

Matt installed locks for which he alone had the key. He feared his mother might wander down the hill to the lake. He'd found that even on her most restless days, he could take her down to the dock to feed the ducks. This activity somehow produced a soothing effect, and she giggled and clucked as the ducks quacked and dived for the bits of bread she threw into the water.

At night after the sleeping sedative had taken its full effect on his mother, Matt would lose himself in his research. Consulting had "worked out", as he had assured Steve. His reputation in the area of aerospace research had followed him from his office at the Center to his technically equipped study at home. He was encouraged to find that associates from laboratories at places such as NASA, McDonnell-Douglas, and General Dynamics still sought his services. The work was his escape, his diversion, the only semblance of sanity in his world.

Then one morning, he went into his mother's room to awaken her. He found her frail, lifeless body lying in a fetal position. He simply bent and kissed her soft, wrinkled cheek. He didn't weep. He was glad. The tortured soul of this once gentle, loving mother person had finally found peace.

The blizzard-like conditions of the night before left the snowy roads covered with a thick crust of ice. Schools and offices would be closed, meetings canceled and the Center opened later in the day, after the Air Force salt trucks did their job. However, the weather made no change in Matt Murray's work schedule. He simply moved to another room of his house to begin work on his latest project, a job from NASA Langley.

Still wearing his robe, he was preceded down the hallway by his two feline companions. The fat cat, called Aslan, had long, fluffy, orange fur. The full orange tail, held proudly erect, resembled a pom-pom being waved by a University of Tennessee cheerleader, thus earning him the nickname, "Big Orange". The cat's companion was long, sleek, and solid black. His name was Spencer. He moved stealthily through the house, crouching behind chairs, and stalking dust balls, leaves, or any debris that had been tracked into the house. He would then pounce upon the prey, as if his only meal of the day depended upon the "kill".

Matt opened the door of his study. It was a large room. One full wall consisted of a sliding glass door that led onto a deck. The woods and lake beyond provided a breath-taking natural mural for a room that otherwise contained an accumulation of metal and plastic high-tech equipment. A computer work station stood against one wall, flanked on one end with a copier and on the other end with a modem and fax machine. The opposite wall held floor to ceiling bookshelves that contained a well-stocked engineering reference library. The end of the room that faced the scenic view was occupied by a large, brown leather recliner and a bronze floor lamp.

Matt checked his fax for data from Langley. No show. Well, that brought his work day to a grinding halt.

The orange and black cats followed him to the kitchen as they anticipated breakfast. Matt cracked a small can of biscuits. Their baking provided him with just enough time to fry two sausage links and four over-lights. He set a plate with two of the eggs on the table. The other two eggs were left in the pan which he placed on the floor. The cats exchanged a few cursory swats before settling down to eat.

Leisurely sipping a third mug of coffee, Matt watched pensively through the kitchen window as squirrels and birds scurried about. They chattered and twittered at the transformation of the woods from winter starkness to the frozen white blanket that now covered their nests and food sources. Matt had a feeling of composure and peace. After years of dealing with sickness, death, teenagers, and even insanity, healing began to take place. As all the pain and anxieties of the last ten years subsided, a sense of serenity and control over his own life grew within him.

After loading the dishwasher, Matt went to his study to check his fax machine. There was still no incoming data. This hitch in his work program left him with a free day. He decided to hike down the hill to check on his neighbor, Ignatius Harder. The severe weather might pose special problems for his friend, who was confined to a wheelchair.

Matt showered first. Soon the bathroom was filled with steam and the sound of an untrained baritone voice. As he completed his wash, Matt threw open the shower curtain to discover two other bathers seated upon the rug. Dampened paws moved across the faces and ears of his unimpressed feline audience. When Matt laughed at their indifference, they simply stood, turned, and walked out. He reached for his electric razor and quickly removed his morning stubble. From a chest in the bedroom, he took a pair of rib-knit cotton thermals and woolen socks. In his closet, he found a pair of full length, black and jade ski pants and a matching down parka. Hiking boots completed his winter attire.

Before leaving the house, Matt made a stop in the kitchen. He snatched a sack of wild bird seed from the pantry shelf to fill the bird feeders before starting down the hill.

CHAPTER 3

Wednesday Morning

Matt's home was located atop a hill overlooking Tims Ford Lake. The road leading to his log house spiraled up a hill and dead ended at a mailbox labeled Murray.

Matt's winter hike proved to be a more arduous activity than he had imagined. It wasn't the seven inches of snow that was so challenging as much as the crust of ice that covered the snow and hampered his progress down the hill. Dogwood and pine trees bowed to touch the ground under the weight of the ice. The limbs of less yielding oak, poplar, and walnut trees snapped and crashed to the ground. Crackling sounds of breaking branches could be heard throughout the woods as Matt made his way down the hill, struggling to stay afoot.

Brilliant sunlight beamed down upon the snow and created a painful glare. Matt's ski sunglasses provided little relief from the dazzle. The ditches on each side of the unpaved road were indistinguishable. Underbrush was hidden and tree limbs reached upward, beseeching the sun to remove their white mantles. Matt loved the beauty of a winter snowstorm. For a short time it transformed the environment into an awesome scene of profound, spectacular beauty.

As he peered through the woods to his right, Matt saw the flashing red and blue lights of an emergency vehicle. He quickened his pace as much as the treacherous footing would allow. He still had to go around the next curve and down to the other side of the hill before he would reach the flashing lights. Matt realized the lights must be located at the Hayes place, just to the right of the next bend in the road.

He slipped and slid over frozen road and rounded the turn. A car marked Franklin County Sheriff stood in front of a mailbox that was colorfully painted with bluebirds, squirrels, and rabbits. It was marked J. R. Hayes. The Sheriff's car was accompanied by two unmarked vehicles, lights flashing on the dashboard. Farther down the hill, an ambulance waited, unable to travel the last few yards up the icy road to the house.

Matt slid to a stop by grabbing the fender of the Sheriff's car. He found himself looking at the backs of two police officers. One officer was tall and broad-shouldered, the other thin and loose-limbed. As they heard the thump of Matt's gloved hand against the car, both men turned, hands poised beside their sidearms. The big man's expression quickly changed from alarm to recognition.

"Matthew! Well now, what the hell are you doing out on a day like this?"

Matt recognized the deep voice spoken in a familiar slow Middle Tennessee accent. "Hey, Ben...Dexter...I might ask you the same thing. What's going on?"

"It appears your neighbor here had herself one God-awful accident," Ben replied.

"What happened?"

"Don't really know myself yet. Just got here. I been up on Monteagle Mountain half the night. Some guy from Indiana thought it was stupid to close I-24 over the mountain just because we had a little winter weather. Tried to show us how to drive in the snow down here. Took half the night to get his car up outta a 50 ft. deep ravine, and the other half of the night to get his dead wife out. Guy's gonna be okay, though. Broken collar bone. Little boy--three years old--not so lucky. Still in Intensive Care at Erlanger. Snow makes some folks crazy."

"Jeez, that's too bad, Ben."

Ben sighed. "Come on up with me if you want to. Just gettin' ready to take a look-see."

Matthew followed Ben and his eager Deputy up the icy drive and toward a clearing in the back of the crab orchard stone house. Dexter talked animatedly to his boss, explaining that the accident had been reported by Ignatius Harder. He had been using binoculars to watch a doe and her twin fawns foraging for food in the clearing. It seemed that the doe led her young within 10 feet of the body. Harder immediately called 911. They'd had a hard time getting up the hill, Dexter declared.

Rounding the house, Matt's eyes suddenly fell upon a scene that he had recently encountered. A sinister feeling of deja vu permeated his senses. His hands felt damp and clammy and sweat appeared above his upper lip. His face was pale. A bitter taste of bile rose to his mouth. He watched in horror as three men moved cautiously on the winter stage, turning his dream into reality.

Ben realized that his friend had stopped and was leaning against a tree.

"Matthew, you okay? Hey, if this is gonna' bother you, go on back down."

Matt found, however, that his trepidation quickly succumbed to curiosity. "I'm okay, Ben. Walking on this ice is just more strenuous than I realized. I'll be fine."

As they stepped into the clearing, the men were joined by three officers. The group moved to a place where scattered logs had been transformed into a smooth white mound by the earlier snow. Their eyes fell upon a blue denim jacket, barely visible through the snow that covered it. A hand, curved in a claw-like manner, thrust upward. Dark hair and fixed brown eyes were set into a frozen face that was barely discernible beneath the ice and snow.

"Would you look at this?" Ben used a conciliatory tone that Matt might use if the cats knocked milk off the table. "What a shame...a pretty thing like this. Matthew, can you identify this woman?"

Matt leaned forward to look at the frozen face smeared with blood. Lifeless eyes stared back at him. He quickly turned away. "Yes, that's my neighbor, Autumn Hayes."

"Ben," said one of the deputies "looks like she came out early this morning to get some firewood. The snow out here is like a solid sheet of ice. See that big rock there?" He pointed to a jagged, blood-caked stone. "It seems like she slipped down hard and hit her head on that. Doc will have to call that one for sure, though. Anyway, them boots she's wearing weren't made to tromp 'round in the snow in."

"Doc, that make sense to you?" asked Ben, turning to look at a red-faced, white haired, overweight man of about sixty.

"I don't know yet. There's a lot to consider here," the doctor answered. "Have to take a closer look back at the lab. Gonna be some trick getting her down to the ambulance, though. Leastwise we don't need to hurry."

"Well," Dexter said, "they sure had a supply of logs. Look at this walnut! Can you believe that? Burning walnut wood in a fireplace! Why, there's woodworkers that would give anything for this mess of wood."

"I remember when they had the wood cut," Matt said. "There were a couple of large walnut trees obstructing their view of the lake. They had someone cut them down and stack the wood back here."

"Dexter," said Ben, "what about all those footprints over there?"

"They're all ours, Sheriff. It must have snowed quite a bit after the accident. Time we got here, there weren't no prints left in the clearing at all, 'cept a few animal prints. We took pictures."

"House is unlocked, I suppose?" asked Ben.

"Yes sir."

"Anybody else here?"

"Well, not exactly. Come on, I'll show you."

Dexter led the way toward a wooden deck that extended from one end of the house to the other. Matt shivered as he ascended steps he had so recently viewed in his dream.

The sight of the curved burgundy sofa placed in front of the fireplace and window did nothing to settle Matt's nerves.

"Well, ain't this something?" Ben glanced around. "She had a real nice place here. Look at that view," he said, looking through the glass door at the lake beyond. "Can understand how some folk would want to cut down any trees obstructing that view, but to use walnut for firewood."

The three men stood silently for a few minutes, glancing about the room. Almost simultaneously, their eyes fell upon a ball of white fluff and pink skin huddled against the black sofa pillows as if trying to hide.

"What in the world have we got here?" crooned Ben. "What kinda animal is that?"

Matt moved toward the dog. "It's a poodle, Ben. He belongs to the Hayeses. I think he's a house dog. Almost never saw him outside."

"But what's wrong with his fur?"

"They had it cut that way...at a grooming parlor, I suppose."

"You mean they deliberately did that to him?"

"Yeah."

Matt bent to touch the dog. The dog let out a soft growl that quickly turned into a whimper. Matt's hand moved closer to him, allowing the dog a sniff before he scratched behind its ear.

"Dexter, you had a chance to talk to anybody around here yet?"

"No sir."

"Matthew, maybe you can help us out a little bit. Tell us what you know about your neighbors here."

"What do you want to know? I really didn't know them well."

"Why don't you start with names."

"The woman's name was Autumn Hayes."

"Autumn Hayes--huh, sounds like a weather front," Ben snickered. "No disrespect intended," he added quickly.

Matt grinned slyly. "I always thought it sounded like the name of a stripper. Anyway, her husband's name is James. Don't know what the R. stands for. They bought this lot and contracted to have the house built. They moved in last spring about April or May. I know they had a cookout on July Fourth. They called it an open house. They invited the neighbors. Only time I ever came inside, but I remembered how nice the place is."

"What does her husband do?"

"He's an engineer out at the Center. We'd worked in some of the same areas, and we'd both worked for the same company back East. Computech."

"You work there at the same time?"

"No. I was there 20 years ago. He's a lot younger than I. His wife worked there, too. Good company to learn the ropes with. Hayes left Computech about a year ago."

"Was she employed now?"

"No. Not that I know of."

"Did you ever see her around during the day?"

"Occasionally when I would jog. Saw her working outside."

"Ever have any conversations?"

"Not really...just 'hello', 'how are you', things like that."

"What about the husband? Ever talk to him?"

"Only real conversation was at the cookout they had. We talked about work, and I asked about mutual acquaintances at Computech."

"They got any family 'round here?"

"I don't know."

"Any idea where the husband is?" Ben continued.

"No."

"Know anyone who could tell us?"

"Might get some information from personnel out at the Center."

"Yeah, I will."

"Sorry. I can't help out more. This is a rotten shame." Matt looked through the glass door as the three men helped the ambulance attendants balance an occupied stretcher across the slippery landscape.

"By the way, Matthew, you never said exactly what it was you were doing out on a day like this."

"Me? Oh, I was just going down to check on Ignatius, see if the weather has posed any problems for him."

"Oh, I see. Still gonna go?"

"Sure. What about this?" Matt asked, pointing to the cowering dog.

"Hell, I don't know," said Ben. "Thing could freeze to death. You willing to take care of it till the husband shows?"

"No, my cats would eat it alive." Matt looked thoughtful. "Suppose we take it down to Ignatius. See if he can take care of it. If he can't, I'll call Dr. Baldwin, the vet over on Short Springs Road."

"Thanks, Matthew." Ben sighed. "I sure don't need to be worried about no animal right now." He stood up and rubbed his red, puffy eyes. "Well, let's go on down to Ignatius' place, see what he can tell us. Dexter, finish here and lock the place up. See you back at the office."

"Yes sir, Sheriff," snapped Dexter, delighted at the authority his newly-assigned duty gave him.

Matt opened his coat. As he reached for the small dog, it whimpered but offered no resistance. Matt curled him into his jacket and quickly closed the zipper. He could feel the pitiful animal's racing heartbeat against his chest.

As they left the house, Ben said, "By the way, Matthew, you know the lady who lives 'cross the road? Mailbox says Phillips."

"Pretty well," said Matt. "She's an older woman, about the same age as my Mother would be. She and Mom used to visit, shop, talk on the phone. Her husband is a maintenance supervisor over at the Center. She doesn't go out much anymore."

As they descended the steps, Matt glanced across the clearing toward the woodpile. The once lovely carpet of snow was now defiled by the tracks of the investigating officers.

"My men tried to talk to Mrs. Phillips, but she wouldn't open the door. Said she couldn't be sure they were policemen. Told them to come back later and talk to her husband. So we'll just wait and talk to him." Ben sighed. "I got enough to worry about today without upsetting an old lady."

As they piled into the Sheriff's car, Matt patted the lump beneath his jacket.

CHAPTER 4

Matt had met Ignatius Harder one summer day soon after Jill's death. Matt had taken his kayak to the Ocoee River to ride the white water. As he was unloading his kayak, a large red van with a handicap sticker pulled into the parking lot, and a red haired, full-bearded, scowling man in a motorized wheelchair came out. Matt was surprised to recognize the man as his new neighbor. He had introduced himself and learned that he had much in common with Ignatius Harder. They were both widowers, engineers, and generally loved the great outdoors and specifically white water rafting and kayaking. When Matt's mother became ill, Ignatius had helped Matt set up his own consulting service similar to the one he operated from his house.

The Sheriff's car skidded to a stop in front of a one-story redwood house. It was situated on a lot at the bottom of the hill.

Matt followed Ben up the snow-covered driveway to the front of the house. The men grasped a handrail as they made their way up the slippery ramp to the front door. Matt banged the iron door knocker. Soon he heard the grind of wheels on wood moving toward the door.

"Who?" boomed a voice.

"Hey, Nate it's me, Matt...and Ben."

"Hey, Matt. Wait a minute."

There was a rattle of locks being unfastened. The door opened to reveal the familiar face of Ignatius Harder, teeth grinning through a mass of red beard.

"Get on in here, guys. It's cold as a well-digger's ass out there."

The two visitors quickly accepted Nate's invitation. Double doors opened into a great room. The kitchen portion of the room was outfitted with appliances and cupboards designed to be used by one sitting in a wheelchair. One wall of the living area was consumed by a four-foot-tall bookshelf, above which hung an oil painting framed in beautiful wood of local origin. A large handmade rag rug covered the floor in front of the blazing stone fireplace. The furniture was also handmade. Above the fireplace was a mantel on which set an antique kitchen clock. Old glass oil lamps stood ready for use. Snapshots and photographs of a laughing face set with green eyes and framed with blonde hair were positioned across the mantel, much as one would prepare an altar for worship.

Several sliding doors were set into the walls, providing access to a deck that completely encircled the house. Beside one glass door stood an easel upon which was fixed a partially finished oil painting of a snowy landscape.

Two smaller rooms and a bathroom completed the floor plan of the house. The bedroom contained a bed outfitted with bars so Ignatius could lift himself from wheelchair to bed. The second room, used as a study, was furnished much like Matt's study with computer, fax, copier, and other equipment necessary to Ignatius' work.

Ben and Matt stamped the snow that stuck to their boots onto a mat imprinted with a picture of three geese winging above a clump of cattails. They followed Ignatius into the welcomed warmth of the great room.

"How you been doing, Nate?" asked Ben.

"I'm fine. Been watching your men bust their asses out there." He pointed to binoculars left on a table by the glass door. "Well, let's have it. Fill me in."

Ben told Ignatius the details, and then added, "And now, Ignatius, wonder if you'd answer a few questions for me...for my report you know."

"Shoot."

Ben cleared his throat. "What's the first thing you did when you got up this morning?"

"Peed!" roared Ignatius. He looked disgusted. "We gonna' have to play twenty questions before I get to tell about this?"

"Okay, okay. Sorry," said Ben. "Just tell me in your own words what you saw."

There was a pause as Ignatius organized his thoughts. "This morning, I was looking..."

"Ah, Ignatius," Ben seemed reluctant to interrupt, "About what time would that have been?"

Ignatius glared at him. "Around 11:00 or 11:30, I suppose. Well, I know it was after the snow stopped. I couldn't have seen much through that snow. Anyway, I was using those binoculars to watch the wildlife. As I was watching a flock of purple finches, a doe stepped right into my sights. Then, when I focused on her, I realized she had two fawns with her. I watched them, oh, fifteen minutes or more, I guess. They moved all along my backyard there and through the trees to that clearing behind the Hayes place. Kept watching them over there and pretty soon the doe walked real close--say 10 feet--from something blue sticking out of the snow. I swear I could see her--the doe--twitching her nose. Then she turned and led her fawns off real quick like--into those woods over there." He pointed. "So I focused my binoculars on whatever it was that had startled the doe. I saw a hand sticking out of a blue coat or sweater or something. Then, I saw the black hair spread all out. And when I focused on her face, I swear it looked like those big, dark eyes were staring right back at me. God! Scared the shit out of me. Tell you the truth, I had to wait two three minutes before I could pick up that phone and dial." He paused.

"Okay now, buddy?" asked Ben with sincere concern.

"Sure, but I'm prepared to see those eyes again...in my dreams."

"Natius, did you see anybody else besides Miz Hayes while you were looking?"

"No, just the animals I mentioned."

"Did you know Autumn Hayes?"

"Not really. I did attend a cookout at their place last July 4. They never came to visit, and I don't go out very much." He slapped the arms of his wheel chair. Ben blushed.

"Know her husband?"

"No, just who he is and that he works at the Center."
"Then you wouldn't know where he is now?"
"No."
"Poor guy." Ben shook his head. "Imagine coming home and finding that your wife is dead. 'Specially gruesome to die like that."
"Know if they have family around here?"
"No."
"Well, I suppose that's all I need to ask you right now. I'm sorry you had to be the one to see this and all. Can I do anything for you?"
"No thanks, Ben. I'm okay. Just one hellava shock to see a woman dead like that." His eyes moved slowly to the pictures on the mantle.
Ben cleared his throat. "Well, I gotta be going. Ain't had no sleep for 36 hours, and don't 'spect I'll get any anytime soon. I tell you what---snow makes some folks crazy."
"By the way, I noticed you got neighbors across the street. No name on the mailbox. Can you tell me who they are?"
"That would be Elizabeth and John Jeffreys. Don't think they're at home though. Both have jobs at the hospital."
"Know when they get home?"
"Usually about 4:30, but with all the emergencies caused by the weather, who knows"
"Right. I'll just catch 'em later."
Ben started toward the door, and then stopped abruptly, as if he remembered something. "Matthew, you

gonna be able to get home? I'm not sure I can get my car all the way up to your place."

"Oh, I'm fine, Ben. Thanks anyway, but I want to talk to Nate for a while.

Ben looked at him disbelievingly. "Whatever, buddy." He flashed his famous smile, walked to the double door, turned up his collar and went outside.

Matt felt a stirring inside his coat. "Good, grief! I forgot...hope he hasn't smothered," he said as he unzipped his jacket. He reached inside and carefully withdrew the pitiful, half-naked, trembling animal.

Ignatius' lower jaw dropped in amazement. "What...who?"

Matt laughed. "It's a dog, Nate. He belongs to the Hayeses." He cradled the animal in the palms of the two big hands that he thrust out as if presenting a gift to his friend. "We couldn't just leave it there, not knowing when Jim Hayes would come in. It appears to be a pretty helpless thing."

"Helpless? That's putting it mildly. What the hell happened to its fur?" Ignatius said, peering more closely.

"He's been clipped. You have it done at a dog grooming parlor."

"Why on earth would anybody do that to a helpless animal?" Ignatius said incredulously.

"I think he's a house dog. Doesn't go outside much."

"Well, if I had something that looked like that, I wouldn't let it outside either."

"Nate, someone has to take care of him until Jim Hayes shows up. We wondered if you'd be willing."

"Why me? Why don't you take it home?"

"Because--you know my cats might just kill it."

"Oh jeez! Well, get a towel outta the bathroom and put it on the rug there in front of the fire. It'll probably die of pneumonia anyway. I'll tell you one thing, Ben owes me. I want you to call a vet to take him if Hayes doesn't get in here tomorrow. This'll teach me not to call 911 again!"

Ignatius' voice trailed off as Matt went into the bathroom to fetch a towel. He returned with a thick oversized tan one that he folded several times. He placed it on the floor and turned up the edges creating a sort of nest. He placed the dog inside. The naked animal circled twice, lay down, and closed its eyes. He appeared to be content for the first time since its ordeal began.

Matt spoke. "I think his name is Pierre."

"Pierre? What kind of a name is that for a dog?"

Matt laughed. "I believe it's French for Peter."

"Peter? That's no better. I'm just gonna call him Pete."

At that, the dog lifted his eyelids and looked straight at Ignatius as if to acknowledge his new name. Then he contentedly closed them again.

"Ignatius, I need to talk to you about something. It's pretty important, at least to me." Matt paused. "The problem is I don't know how or where to begin."

"The only time you call me Ignatius, instead of Nate, is when it's something *important*." Ignatius moved to the kitchen. "Why don't I make up a couple of cups of coffee and a little Jack for you while you tell me about it?"

Matt could hear the sounds of the coffee maker. Soon, his host returned in his motorized wheelchair. He held a coffee pot in one hand and a pint of black label Jack

Daniels lay in his lap. The round oak table in the center of the room held several mugs. Ignatius filled two with the steaming, dark brew and then splashed a generous amount of whiskey into Matt's mug. He took his black, without whiskey.

"Okay, Matt, try this and let's hear what's up."

The steaming hot concoction soon warmed Matt. He began to relax as his mind wandered back over the events of the morning. Ignatius waited patiently as his friend organized his thoughts.

"Nate, did you ever have a dream and then, later on, that dream came true?"

Ignatius looked thoughtful. "No, Matt, can't say as I have. Have you?"

"Yes, I have. And it's happened more than once. Oh, I don't mean that everything I dream comes true. Hell, if it did, I wouldn't go to sleep." He laughed nervously. Nate nodded. "But I've had a dream, and then the dream would happen. This has happened several times."

Ignatius lifted his mug. "Tell me about some of these dreams."

"There are really just three that are vivid. I mean, I know for sure that there was a dream, and then it happened. And sometimes I have this deja vu feeling. I wonder if I could have dreamed this, too."

"I've read that lots of people have the feeling of deja vu, Matt. Tell me about the dreams."

"The first was when the twins were about a year or maybe a year and a half old. They had just started walking. They walked real young, you know, and they also had learned to climb out of their stroller. Anyway, one Saturday

Jill took them to Walmart, and she took the stroller to push them in." Matt was becoming nervous. "I stayed home to cut the grass. About an hour later, Jill came in, all upset and crying. While she was at the store, she turned her back and Garth climbed out of the stroller and disappeared. When she realized what had happened, she had everyone in the store looking for him. A clerk found him behind a counter taking shoes out of the boxes. He sat there surrounded by shoes. The search had lasted about 15 minutes, and they'd even locked the doors, not allowing anyone to leave, until they found him. Jill was hysterical. Then, while Jill was telling me this, I remembered--that I had dreamed this. Down to the shoes scattered on the floor. I don't mind telling you, I was really spooked."

Ignatius was silent for a while. "Did you tell Jill?"

"Hell, no. I didn't want her to think she was married to some kind of freak."

"You said there was another dream."

"Yes. In this other dream, there's Chad, Garth, and me. The boys are older, like school age. We're standing on a little hill looking down at this crowd of people milling about. I recognize my mother as one of the people in the crowd. She shakes hands with people and then walks toward this big, black car. Then several months later, I am standing on that same hill with Garth and Chad, looking down at the same crowd of people. My mother was walking around and shaking hands with people and thanking them. It wasn't until I stood there in the cemetery watching my mother move toward the black limo that I realized I'd dreamed about Jill's funeral."

Matthew Murray suddenly fell silent. Only the ticking of the mantel clock broke the stillness as both men grappled with Matt's bizarre story. Matt looked across the table at his friend. Ignatius' red bushy eyebrows and scraggy beard masked a shrewd, yet compassionate mind.

He set his mug upon the table. "That's two. You said there were three that you could distinctly remember."

"Yes." Matt leaned forward, arms supporting him on the table. "The third one was last night."

Ignatius' eyes narrowed

Matt continued. "Last night I dreamed about Autumn Hayes dying. I dreamed the whole thing, Nate. I swear, it was just as if I were in her house--on the stairs and looking down at the living room and out onto the back clearing. I saw it all." His words were faster, more slurred. "I even saw him." Matt pointed to the dog. "I swear it was just like I was watching a movie when the whole thing happened."

Ignatius said, "You dreamed about Autumn Hayes' accident?"

"No, Nate!" Matt said hoarsely. "I dreamed about Autumn Hayes' _murder_!" He pushed back his chair abruptly and walked to face the glass door that looked out into the snowy woods. His shoulders rose and fell.

Some time passed before Ignatius broke the silence. "Matt, why don't you tell me about the one you had last night?"

Matt turned to face Ignatius, then walked back to his chair. He poured himself another cup of coffee, splashed in some whiskey, and sat down. He stared into the cup as if it were a crystal ball. After two big gulps, he continued his revelation, describing all the details of the dream.

For a long time, the men sat staring at each other, neither knowing what to say. Matt finally broke the silence. "I don't know what to do. I can't tell Ben about this. Hell, he'd think I'm crazy. On the other hand, this morning when the officers were describing what they thought had happened, I wanted to scream---that's not the way she died. It was no accident. Someone came out of that stand of dogwood trees and picked up a rock and bashed her head in." Matt wiped his sweating forehead with the sleeve of his down jacket. "So what do I do?"

"Matt, now take it easy. Calm down. You said yourself that not all of your dreams come to pass. Just because you dreamed a murder doesn't mean it was really a murder."

"Nate, what are the chances that I dreamed all the events of her death accurately except for the murder part? I don't think so. I've never had an experience where only half the dream actually happened."

"Okay, try this. Suppose you're only half awake, and you stumble over to the window, see the snow, and observe Autumn Hayes going to her woodpile to get logs. You fall back in bed, go to sleep again, and put your own ending to what you think is the beginning of a dream. Meantime, Autumn has an accident, dies, and you think you've dreamed the whole thing."

"Couldn't happen."

"Why not?"

"Because I can't see the Hayes' clearing from any window in my house. What am I going to do? If only Ben and his men hadn't seemed so sure it was an accident. If only there was some way to raise a question without making me look like some kind of fortune teller-type freak."

"Or worse, without making you look like a suspect." Ignatius pulled himself closer to the table. "After all, you're the only one questioning the cause of death."

"Would I do that if I'd killed her?"

"Murderers have all kinds of weird behaviors. Publicity seekers. Some of them try to get caught in order to be punished. Hell, no one understands the reasoning of some of these psychotic murderers today."

"Thanks Nate. You've not only raised the possibility that I'm a murderer you've also labeled me a psycho. Not exactly the kind of support I had in mind." Matt slipped his chair away from the table and pushed himself upright. He began to pace back and forth in front of the glass door.

Outside, low-hanging gray clouds again filled the sky, obscuring the sun and suggesting an omen of yet more snow. The bare branches of the trees created an illusion of thrashing arms waving savagely at the house.

Nate spoke softly. "I'm just trying to point out to you, Matt, the kinds of questions that could be raised if you open this can of worms."

Matt licked his lips. "You're right, Nate. I guess I knew this is the kind of thing you should just try to forget. Thanks for listening. It's good to be able to tell someone."

"Right. Now--I've got a Hungarian Goulash in the crock pot. It's been on all day. A little cornbread and a fresh pot of coffee would taste awfully good."

"Sounds great...I didn't realize I was so hungry. I'll help."

The two men went into the kitchen area. As Ignatius made a skillet of Mexican cornbread, Matt collected dishes and condiments. When at last Ignatius brought the crock pot to the round table, Pete lifted his head, sniffed, stood up, and slowly trotted across the room. This was the first sign of life the dog had shown in hours.

CHAPTER 5

At half past four, it was already dark. Matt made his way back up the hill towards his house. Snow was again falling softly.

The snow on the Jeffreys' driveway displayed car tracks that disappeared into a two-car garage. A sixteen-year-old boy sought refuge in a corner bedroom of the house. The tan walls of his room were covered with posters displaying distorted faces of rock stars. An electric guitar rested in a corner next to an expensive high power rack system with CDs and surround sound speakers. The 15" color TV was turned to the MTV channel, where a golden-haired girl dressed in a white and gold toga, danced seductively. Sean Jeffreys sat upon his bed, one leg bent, foot propped on the mattress. His forehead rested on his knee. He rocked and shook as tears rushed down his cheeks. The boy listened as the angry voices of his parents filtered through the thin walls of the house.

"You expect me to be sorry she's dead? A selfish little bitch, who only cared about herself, proving to herself how cute she was, how desirable she was? Not caring what she did to hurt other people? You really expect me to be sorry?" Elizabeth Jeffreys' voice was mocking and sarcastic.

"For God's sake, Liz. The woman's dead. Just let it go."

"It'll be a long time before I can just let it go, John. Just how long do you think I should allow myself to remember someone who pretended to be a good neighbor, ingratiated herself to our son, and used husbands for some kind of egocentric escapade? And I am supposed to be sorry she's dead, unable to hurt anyone else. I'll not be a hypocrite, John. I only wish she could die twice. Nothing that happened to her is enough retribution for what she's done."

"Liz, you're hysterical. Shut up! You want the whole hill to hear you?"

"I don't care who hears me. I hate the thought of her dying with some people thinking what a *kind, sweet, nice, helpful* neighbor she was. She was wicked, wicked, John. A back stabber. Worming her way into situations, just so she could use people, enjoying manipulating..."

Sean slapped his hands over his ears.

There were no street lights on the roadside, yet Matt moved unimpeded up the familiar hill. As he rounded the curve to his left, he saw that Mr. Phillips had parked his blue Nissan truck on the street in front of his mailbox, thus avoiding the possibility of being stuck in his driveway the next morning. Lights from the house could be seen through the snowfall, giving a feeling of reassurance and warmth.

Then suddenly, some instinct of movement caused Matt to jerk his head in the direction of the Hayes place. The house stood dark, hushed, foreboding. The windows looked like slabs of shiny black marble embedded in the side of the house. Then suddenly, a small light darted back and forth across a window. Matt watched, dumbfounded, as the flicker of illumination began to move from room to room.

Perhaps Dexter was doing one last walk-through to make sure everything was locked up. But why not just turn on the lights? The light disappeared, and the house returned to darkness. Matt listened intently for the door to open and close, but there was only silence. It seemed like an eternity of waiting in the darkness. How long should it take for someone to walk from the house to the road?

It was then that he realized there was no law enforcement vehicles parked in front of the house. Matt suddenly felt vulnerable. Then he heard a sound, a crunching of foot on snow, slowly, and stealthily. Matt could feel the pressure of his heart as it pounded against the wall of his chest. It was then that he remembered the flashlight Ignatius had handed him as he left his house. Reaching under his parka, he pulled the light from his hip pocket. His gloves made the task more difficult, and the metal cylinder slid through his hand and clattered to the snow. He could hear it roll on the icy crust. Damn! At that moment a flurry of movement sounded in the brush beside the Hayes driveway.

"Who's there?" barked Matt.

His mouth was dry, hands trembling. He fell to his knees, patting the snow in an effort to locate the flashlight. Finally, his hand touched the light. As he pushed the switch, a beam of light fixed on a pair of large, brown, frightened eyes. The illuminated head suddenly jerked back and turned as the doe scurried out of the brush and across the road to the safety of the woods beyond.

Matt wiped the perspiration from his forehead and followed the beam of his flashlight as he slowly trudged up the hill.

As he unlocked the door to his house, Matt heard the two cats, Aslan and Spencer, jump from some favorite perch. Soon he felt their warm greeting as the animals rubbed their furry bodies against his legs.

"Hi, guys," Matt said as he removed his parka and gloves. "Bet you're hungry."

He followed the cats as they pranced, tails erect, towards the kitchen. Matt removed two small cat dinners from the pantry shelf.

"How about shrimp and chicken delight tonight?" he asked as he attached one can to the clamp of the electric can opener. The cats responded to the whirring sound of the appliance by hissing and swatting at each other. Soon two saucers of the stinking concoction were being devoured by the contented cats.

Matt sat at his kitchen table sipping hot chocolate, and trying to make sense of the day's events. He was relieved to have shared the dream with Nate, and he felt okay about the decision not to discuss it with Ben. Matt accepted that he didn't understand the phenomenon, but hell; there were lots of inexplicable things in this world. There was, however, one question he'd be sure to ask Ben... who the hell was snooping around the Hayes house in the dark with a flashlight?

The silence was broken by the ringing of the phone. Matt lifted the receiver and pulled up the antenna of the cordless instrument.

"Yeah?"

"Matt," Ignatius said, "forget about calling that vet in the morning. Hell, this naked mutt could freeze to death being hauled in and out in this weather. You want that on your conscience?"

"No, Nate." Matt smiled. "I surely don't want that on my conscience."

Just before the line clicked silent, Matt thought he heard a sharp, shrill yap in the background.

CHAPTER 6

Thursday Morning

The meteorologist on the national weather channel was informing her viewers that the winter weather "event" they were experiencing was the worst snowstorm to hit the Southeast in a century. She reported that travel throughout the eastern third of the nation was at a virtual standstill. A list of airport delays rolled across the screen. Busses and trains were not moving. A map appeared showing a white strip from Alabama to Maine. Winds of up to 65 miles per hour were reported along the east coast. High waves lashed the Atlantic shore and small craft warnings were in effect from South Carolina to Massachusetts.

Outside, the wind blew drifts of snow three feet deep. Limbs snapped under the weight of the ice. Matt waited to hear what the snow accumulation was for other Tennessee cities. It was still snowing. Apparently, the storm, which was moving in from the southwest, was taking its time in its trip across the country.

Matt doubted that Langley would be sending any data today. It appeared that Virginians would have as much difficulty getting to jobs as the rest of the east. A check of his fax machine verified his assumption.

Matt needed to focus on something tangible. He reviewed the printouts on his desk. Then, moving to his work station, he ran his computer program to generate another set of predictions varying a different parameter. As he was examining the plot output from one of these cases, he glanced out of the sliding glass door into the snowy woods. Four brilliant red male cardinals vied for the territory around the newly-stocked bird feeders, while four contented females ate hungrily. Two doves pecked at the snow onto which seed had spilled. There were also snow birds, tit mice, chickadees, and nut hatches. What a variety of hungry little beggars, Matt thought, and what a contrast the peaceful winter scene presented to the high tech plastic and metal office.

Matt's reverie was interrupted by the telephone.
"Yeah?"
"Hey, Matthew. Ben. How's it going? Well, you folks up there had enough excitement yesterday to last you for a while. I'm down here at Doc Turner's lab, and we've come up with some things that I need to get some answers to. Now, I know we got ourselves a blizzard out there, but this here is something I feel like we need to get on right away."
"Uh huh."
"What's the chances, Matthew, of you getting down that hill to 'Natius' place? You see, I'm driving my own four-wheel-drive now. The winds blowing so hard, a couple of four-wheel-drive vehicles are stuck right there at the bottom of your hill. Some fool kids were gonna get out and help people who were in trouble. Ended up in a mess themselves. Well, anyway, I can drive my vehicle to where they're stuck, and then I'll walk on over to Nate's place. Think you can make it there?"

"Sure, I think so. This must be pretty important, Ben."

"Yeah, it is, Matthew. Time might be real important here. I'll explain when I see you."

"Okay, Ben. Take care now."

"You too buddy. I'll give Ignatius a call. Tell him we're coming."

Nothing had prepared Matt for the bitter wind that cut through his ski parka and pants. The wind lifted blowing sheets of snow into the air and threw it against him. His green clothing was soon white. The heavy gale pushed hard against his body as if trying to deter him from his meeting with the Sheriff. The roads and paths were completely hidden and drifts gave misleading clues to curves and ditches. Matt maneuvered his way down the hill as much by instinct as by sight. He was hardly aware when he passed his neighbors' houses, so intent was he upon reaching his destination as quickly as possible.

Soon the redwood house appeared through the storm. Matthew struggled the last few feet up the ramp and onto the porch. His gloved hand numbly grasped the iron door knocker. The echo of his pounding could be heard from inside. Soon the familiar sound of the grind of wheels on wood could be heard, along with a yapping bark and the click of canine toenails on wooden floors. A gust of wind assisted Ignatius Harder as he opened the door to admit his friend along with a flurry of snow.

"Matt! Get on in here. What the hell's Ben thinking of? Nobody needs to be out in this."

"You can say that again. This better be damned important!" Matt swore.

"Well, come on in here and get those wet clothes off. I got a fresh pot of coffee. And believe it or not, I baked some whole grain bread today. Great hobby, cooking."

Matt smiled and walked toward the inviting fireplace. He removed his parka and gloves and hung them on the back of a chair to dry. Extending his hands toward the fire, he rubbed feeling back into his numb fingers. As he turned, his face took on a shocked expression. Sitting on the floor, tongue extended, was Pete. The poodle was wearing a homemade dog coat fashioned after a horse blanket. A small hand towel had been laid lengthwise on his back and fastened across his stomach with four large safety pins.

Matt burst out laughing. "What you got there, Pete?"

"He's got a coat," answered Ignatius. "What do you think? Somebody stole his natural one." The dog seemed to grin at all this attention. He allowed Matt to pat him gently on the head.

"Well, Nate," said Matt, "what do you suppose this is all about?"

"Haven't the faintest." said Ignatius as he wheeled from the kitchen--coffee pot in hand. He poured two steaming cups of brew and cut thick slices of hot bread. Real butter and wild strawberry preserves were already on the table.

As if avoiding the topic of Autumn Hayes' death would deny its reality, conversation revolved around the blizzard. Each man related tragic and heroic stories they had heard on television and the radio. They discussed reported statistics of snowfall, wind velocity, and storm movement patterns. It was being called the blizzard of the century.

Finally, a loud knock on the door announced that Ben had indeed made it in spite of the rapidly accumulating drifts. As Ignatius unfastened the lock, Ben burst through the doorway.

The men settled themselves in front of the blazing fire. Matt choose a comfortable, stuffed chair and lifted his feet onto the matching footstool. Ben backed up to the fireplace, hands behind his back in search of warmth. He viewed his audience of two intently.

"All right, Ben," snapped Ignatius, "let's have it. This better be damned good."

"Ignatius, I never said it was good. Good certainly don't go with murder."

Nate's jaw dropped, and his eyes widened. Matt turned pale. He could feel his heart begin to race. The silence in the room became unbearable. Finally, Ben spoke again. The blast of his voice masked the ringing in Matt's ears.

"That's right gentlemen. Miz Hayes didn't die in an accident. It appears that your neighbor got herself murdered."

Matthew and Ignatius did not dare to look at each other.

"What makes you think that, Ben?" Matt said. "Yesterday you seemed to be so sure of what happened. You seemed satisfied that Autumn slipped on the ice and struck her head on that rock. What made you change your mind?"

"Once we got the body back to the lab, we found there was actually two pieces of evidence that led us to believe that she was murdered," Ben explained.

Matthew and Ignatius looked at each other. Nate's incredulous look seemed to transmit a message to Matt: "Be careful what you say, he could be digging."

"What kind of evidence?" asked Matt.

"Autumn Hayes died from massive damage to the top of her head. The wounds were inflicted by blows from that large jagged rock we found." Satisfaction radiated from his face. He looked from one man to the other as if anticipating applause. However, two pairs of confused eyes stared back at him as if he were completely mad.

"Wound*s*!" Ben said again. "Don't you get it? Wound*s*...more than one. Autumn Hayes' death resulted from *two* massive wounds to the top of her head." He stepped closer to the two men. "We found that rock by the body. It was covered with blood. We assumed she'd fallen and struck her head on it. When we got back to the lab, Doc Turner confirmed that it was her blood on the rock. The kicker, however, was that Autumn Hayes had not just one, but two injuries on her head. Now assuming that she didn't fall down; hit her head; get up and fall down again, hitting her head on the same rock a second time, then someone inflicted those wounds." Ben paused as if to allow this information a chance to sink in.

He continued, "That, my friends, makes this a murder...not an accident."

Ignatius peered at his friend incredulously. "Ben, I don't know about this."

"You forget," Ben went on, "I said there were two pieces of evidence that make it obvious that she was murdered. The second clue was the location of the wounds." He lifted his right hand and with his finger tapped the top of his head. "Here. Right here. The blows were to the top of her head. If a person fell, it stands to reason that the damage would be done to the side of the head. Autumn Hayes died from blows that were inflicted to the top of her head. There's no doubt. She was struck TWICE on the TOP of her head. Consequently, we've got ourselves a murder here." His right fist slapped into his left palm.

CHAPTER 7

On that snowy March day, Ben discussed the evidence in Autumn Hayes' death as Matt and Nate listened intently. They had been Ben's two strongest supporters when he ran for Sheriff of Franklin County. Now, Ben's keen instinct and attention to detail demonstrated that their confidence in him had not been misplaced. The three friends batted the evidence back and forth, testing its credibility. Yet at no time did Matt mention his dream, which had now obviously entered the realm of reality.

"You've convinced me that an investigation into Autumn Hayes' death is necessary," said Matt. "Where do you go from here?"

"The first thing I want to do," replied Ben, "is find out all I can about the victim, Autumn Hayes. The next thing I'll do is put a check on anyone who had a motive."

"Motive?'

"Yeah. The majority of murders are committed by family or close friends. So first off, I aim to find out all I can about J. R. Hayes."

"Hayes?"

"I called Mildred Prentiss. She works out in Personnel at the Center. Told her Miz Hayes had died, and that I was trying to reach the husband. She gave me the home phone number of his branch manager. He said that Hayes had gone to Buffalo on company business. He was supposed to have returned Tuesday evening."

"I guessed he might be on a business trip," Matt said.

"What made you think that?" asked Ben.

"Nothing specifically. Just a guess."

"Well, you guessed right. Anyway, Hayes' plane landed at Nashville International Airport at 9:30 p.m. on Tuesday." Ben referred to a small spiral note pad he'd taken from his pocket. "I checked with American Airlines, and he was on board, or at least someone claiming to be him. Also, a check of the airport long-term parking area showed his vehicle was no longer parked there."

"What about the storm, Ben?" asked Ignatius. "How was travel between here and Nashville at that time?"

"As best I can determine," Ben said, "It started snowing here around 5:30 p.m. on Tuesday. Nashville hasn't gotten the brunt of the storm like cities farther South and west. So, when it started snowing in Nashville at 8:30 p.m., it wasn't too heavy. By 9:30, landing time for Hayes, there was very little accumulation. Hayes picks up his vehicle and drives on south...toward the storm and possibly on home."

"Now wait a minute, Ben," Matt interrupted. "Didn't you tell me I-24 was closed from just South of Nashville all the way to Chattanooga?"

"Yeah sure, Matt. But it was closed later that night, about 10 or 10:30. Hayes could have passed the road block before then."

Nate spoke. "Even if he did get through before the road block went up, you gonna try to tell us someone drove 90 miles in that storm, arrived home, killed his wife the next morning, and then fled back out into a blizzard? No, I don't think so."

"Now just wait up 'Natius. I ain't through. First off, Hayes wasn't driving just any vehicle. He had a Jeep Cherokee. Second, I had Penny check the motels most easily accessible to I-24 from Murfreesboro to Franklin County exit. Ain't no J. R. Hayes, Jim Hayes, James Hayes, or anyone with a similar name registered at any of these motels. Today's Thursday, a day and a half after Hayes' plane landed in Nashville. How come he hasn't shown up somewhere or at least called? Dexter was at the Hayes house all day Wednesday, and he's sitting there now. No call from Hayes. I got a murdered woman and an unaccounted-for husband. And until I can account for the husband's whereabouts, I'm treating him as a possible suspect."

Ben seemed pleased with his presentation. It appeared that the Sheriff had covered a lot of detail in a short time.

"So, what I'd like to do next," Ben continued, "is try to find out as much about the victim as I can. Matt, I'd like to talk to some of the other neighbors. Maybe they can tell me more than you two can. Would you mind tagging along? It might make folks feel less threatened if a neighbor is with me, especially old Miz Phillips. Couldn't even get her to open the door the other day."

"Sure, Ben. Wanta go now?"

"Yeah, the sooner, the better. Weather report says this storm is supposed to move on out tonight, but what do they know? No sense waiting for a spring thaw."

The two men began the chore of putting on their layers of winter garments, a task accompanied by much grunting and squirming. As they struggled into the clothes,

Matt said, "Ben, I'm glad you mentioned that Dexter had been posted at the Hayes house to take telephone calls. I really got a fright last night as I was walking back up to my place. When I passed the Hayes house, it seemed so quiet and dark. Then I saw Dexter's flashlight through the window, moving from room to room. It was eerie. Then, when a deer jumped out of the brush, I thought I'd have a heart attack."

Ben stopped. He held a boot poised to slip on. His eyes narrowed as he spoke hoarsely, "Matthew, what time was that?"

"Oh, about quarter to 5. It was pitch dark, though." Matt looked up, aware of the intensity of Ben's question. "Why do you ask?"

"Because, you didn't see Dexter in the Hayes house with a flashlight. Dexter left the Hayes in plenty of time to get down this hill before dark. Dexter was in my office at 3:45."

"Then who..."

"I don't know, Matt. But right now I think it's more important than ever to talk to your neighbors."

Ignatius followed the two men to the door. When Matt looked at him, Ignatius said, "Matt, call me tonight when you get home."

"Okay."

"And Matt..."

"Yeah?"

"Be careful." The warning seemed to carry a double meaning. But Matt had no intention of sharing his dream with Ben, certainly not now.

CHAPTER 8

Ben and Matt slid across the road to the Jeffreys' home. Grasping the metal rail, they climbed up four glazed steps to the front porch. Their cautious ascent provided them with enough time to hear raised voices from inside the white brick house. Although the words were indiscernible, the tones were harsh and anxious. As the doorbell buzzed, a loud "Sh-h" from within was followed by silence. Finally, the sound of footsteps could be heard, and the front door was thrown open.

John Jeffreys was a small-framed man of about 5'8". He was meticulously dressed in a single-breasted navy blue suit of the best wool. A crisp white shirt was tucked into the double pleated pants. Highly polished fourteen karat gold cuff links engraved with the letter J peeked out from beneath the coat sleeves. His black wing tip shoes were polished to a lustrous sheen, and the Italian silk tie that was knotted about his neck flashed a daring splotch of red in contrast to the otherwise conservative wardrobe.

"Sheriff, Matt. Do come on in."

"Thanks, Mr. Jeffreys," said Ben.

"It's really cold out here," said Matt, quickly closing the door behind him. "John, I don't know if you've ever met my friend. This is Sheriff Benjamin Day. Sheriff, John Jeffreys. The Sheriff asked me to come along and introduce him to the neighbors."

Ben extended a hand, "Call me Ben, Mr. Jeffreys." They shook hands.

"And just call me John, Sheriff...Ben. We heard about the accident at the Hayes'. So tragic!"

"Yeah, it sure was," said Ben. "Real bad. That's what I came to talk to you about, John. Wondered if you could help us out a little."

At that moment, Elizabeth Jeffreys entered the hall from the kitchen. Elizabeth was as drab in her appearance as Jim was flamboyant. She wasn't really fat, but all the muscles in her body appeared to sag. Her chin and stomach were thrust forward in an effort to balance her tall frame. She had no defined hairstyle, but dry brittle ends and graying roots were evidence that she had once visited a hair dresser. The navy blue, double-knit polyester housedress was out of style, but clean and unwrinkled. She spoke in a poised, arresting voice that seemed inconsistent with her appearance. The Jeffreys couple reminded Matt of a pair of cardinals. The male was bright red, chipper, and twittering. The female was dull and unobtrusive.

"Who is it, John?"

"Matthew Murray and Sheriff Ben Day. Ben, my wife, Elizabeth."

Elizabeth stepped forward and gave Ben's hand one firm pump. "Sheriff."

"The Sheriff is here about the Hayes accident, Elizabeth. He wants to ask us some questions."

Elizabeth did not speak, nor did her expression change.

"Our biggest problem right now," said Ben, "is that we can't seem to locate Mr. Hayes or any of Miz Hayes' family. Have either of you seen or heard from Mr. Hayes since his wife's death?"

"No, Ben. We've been pretty well snowed in," John Jeffreys replied.

"Any idea about Miz Hayes' family? Do you know any of her relatives or how to get in touch with them?"

"No, to both questions, Ben," answered John Jeffreys.

"Did either of you see anyone over at the Hayeses' last evening--after my Deputy left there--after say quarter till four?"

Jeffreys shook his head as he answered. "No, we surely didn't notice anyone over there."

"I hope you folks will understand that these questions are just routine. Now, did the Hayeses get along okay? I mean, any fights, arguments that you're aware of?"

"None that we are aware of."

Ben had not appeared to notice that Elizabeth Jeffreys was making no responses. But now he turned to face her squarely and asked, "Mrs. Jeffreys, I wonder if you could tell me anything about Miz Hayes that might help in locating her family?"

"No, Sheriff," was the reply. "I wasn't a close friend--just a neighbor."

"I see. Can you tell me who some of her close friends might be?"

"No, sorry."

"Know what she might have done for hobbies, recreation?"

"No, Sheriff. I'm sure we didn't have the same interests."

"How do you know that, Mam?"

"We had nothing in common." Elizabeth said flatly.

"But if you didn't know her, how do you know you had nothing in common?"

Elizabeth did not appear to be the least bit ruffled, but John interjected, "Elizabeth and I spent a day at the Hayeses' back in the summer. Matt, you were there. Wasn't it in July? Anyway, the Hayeses were new to the neighborhood and invited us all for a barbecue. It was very nice actually. Elizabeth and I met Autumn then, of course. But since Elizabeth works all day at the hospital, she and Autumn never developed a close friendship."

"I see. Is that right, Miz Jeffreys?"

"Yes, Sheriff. We didn't develop a close friendship."

"Well, I sure would appreciate it if you'd let me know if you think of anything that would help us locate her family. The roads are awfully rough out there. If you must go out, I'd really take all precautions. Got a mess at the bottom of the hill. Some four-wheel-drive vehicles are stuck. You are going out aren't you? Noticed you're all dressed up," Ben said looking at John Jeffreys.

"Oh, yes, Ben. I'm going to the hospital. Admissions keep coming in and some employees are unable to get to work. So anyone who can make it is working today," explained John Jeffreys, "Elizabeth is staying here."

"I see. Well, you be careful, now."

As Ben spoke, Sean Jeffreys stealthily crossed the living room and entered the kitchen. His movements were so silent that one might have questioned whether he had actually passed through the room.

"My son, Sean," John said, as if verifying that they had not seen an apparition.

"Didn't realize you had a son, John. Wonder if he could tell us anything."

"No, Ben. Please, not now. Sean is rather upset." Ben raised an eyebrow. John continued, "You see, we've raised him to feel secure, safe in his own home, and now he realizes that this isn't necessarily true." Ben frowned. John went on. "What I mean is that he realizes now that accidents can happen anywhere, and he has been upset."

"I understand that," Ben sounded reassuring, "but maybe later on, I would like to talk to him."

"Well, if you really think it's necessary."

"Yes, I think it's necessary, John. You see, it appears like Mrs. Hayes' death was not an accident. We think it was murder."

John Jeffreys' jaw dropped, and his eyes bulged. Elizabeth Jeffreys did not change her expression. From the kitchen came the sound of shattering glass.

CHAPTER 9

Matt used the time it took to walk from the Jeffreys' house to fill Ben in on what he knew about his neighbor, Jesse Phillips. He explained that Phillips was a local man whose family had lived in Franklin County for generations. As a matter of fact, Jesse's father had owned many acres of pasture land along the Elk River. When it was decided to dam the river for flood control and to generate electricity, old Mr. Phillips and other farmers had fought the decision vehemently. However, TVA prevailed, and now acres of fine grazing land lay submerged in water on which avid fishermen and audacious water skiers vied for space to pursue their favorite pastimes. Old Mr. Phillips was delighted to discover that some of his land had been spared by the flood waters, and an awesome view of the newly created Tims Ford Lake had endowed him with a very valuable piece of real estate. When Jesse Phillips inherited the land, he immediately took advantage of the demand for lake property, and the hill had quickly developed into a scenic subdivision.

Jesse was a cold war fanatic. He even admired the late Joe McCarthy, and he had videotaped Jesse Helms as he delivered some of his most passionate warnings of communist takeover made possible by the bungling of "self-styled liberals." Phillips was convinced that Oak Ridge and the Center would make Tennessee a target for nuclear missile attacks, so in the early 1960's, he had built a fallout shelter behind his house. The structure consisted of tons of concrete blocks and cement laid deep inside the rocky earth. Its location could be detected only by a large metal ventilation pipe protruding from the earth. The shelter was equipped with water, food, medical kits, blankets, cots, a battery-operated radio, and most importantly, a shotgun. This last item was to insure that only those sanctioned by Jesse Phillips would enter this ark of protection against a nuclear holocaust. Matt remembered that Jesse had extended an invitation to him and his family in the event such a catastrophe should occur. This had been a long time ago, and now weeds hid the metal ventilation pipe.

"Sounds like a weirdo to me," said Ben.

"No, he's really all right," assured Matt. "Mrs. Phillips spent many an hour sitting with Mom so I could have some relief. She'd cook meals and bring them over, and Jesse would run errands and help me keep the place up. They're a little strange, but they're good neighbors."

When his neighbor responded to the door chime, nothing could have prepared Matt for the appearance of the man standing there shivering against the cold. Puffy dark circles appeared under Jesse Phillips' eyes, and sharp wrinkles etched his face. Grimy thermal underwear peeped from under the neck of a red plaid flannel shirt. The legs of the faded jeans were tucked into cowboy boots with the heels so worn that Jesse Phillips appeared to be walking on the sides of his feet. The cadaverous man who beckoned them inside was in sharp contrast to the hearty, strapping neighbor who had accompanied his wife when she visited Matt's mother.

Ben and Matt followed Phillips into a den. It was a comfortable, attractive room, but signs of neglect could be detected from the piles of old magazines, junk mail, and perishing plants in the bay window. Jesse Phillips motioned his guests to sit down. He appeared to be oblivious to loud music assaulting them from the living room across the hall. Matt recognized the voices of a country music gospel quartet as they harmonized, "Whispering hope, whispering hope. Like the song of the angels..."

Matt said loudly, "Mr. Phillips, do you know Ben Day, our Sheriff?"

"Sure, I do. How are you, Sheriff? I've been watching you all work. Know it's been real hard getting 'round in the snow. Weather's suppose to improve this weekend."

"Let's hope so," said Ben. "Mr. Phillips, I suppose you know why I'm here. Your neighbor, Miz Autumn Hayes, died yesterday. And since this wasn't a natural death, I have to ask a few questions. Think you could help me out?"

"Well, don't know if I can help, Sheriff, but I'll be glad to answer some questions."

"Thank you. First off, we haven't been able to locate Mr. Hayes. He hasn't been notified of his wife's death. Do you have any thoughts on how we might catch up with him?"

"No Sheriff, I really haven't. I've had so many personal responsibilities lately that I haven't kept up with my neighbors very well."

"I see. Well, we feel somebody in the family should be notified as soon as possible. Ever hear tell of Autumn Hayes having any family around here?"

"I wouldn't know, Sheriff."

"Now, just strictly for the record, do you know whether or not the Hayeses got along okay? I mean...any fights, you know of?"

"Nope."

"Mr. Phillips, we stopped over here yesterday to talk to your wife. Hope we didn't upset her. I wonder if she might be willing to answer some questions for me now, your being at home and all."

Mr. Phillips let out a deep sigh and looked down at his tightly-locked fingers, "Sheriff, if it isn't absolutely necessary, I wish you wouldn't. The personal responsibility I referred to a few minutes ago is my wife." He nodded in the direction of the loud music. The same song was being played over and over "...Whispering Hope...Jesus thy love...is sweet music."

"You see, my wife is very ill." He looked at Matt as if her sickness created a special bond of understanding between the two men. "She's been real apprehensive, depressed, and agitated. Walks around twisting a Kleenex and listening to gospel music. When she's not listening to that music, she tunes in the TV to one of those television evangelist programs. All of a sudden, she thinks she's a *big* sinner. A kinder, more giving person never lived. You know that, Matt." Matt nodded in agreement.

"Thinks we're both gonna die, or worse, have cancer and suffer a long time," Phillips continued. "Won't go anywhere, or let anyone come here if she's alone. That's why she wouldn't admit you the other day, Sheriff."

Matt's eyes filled with pity. "Mr. Phillips, I had no idea. I'm so sorry. When did this start? Do you think she may have Alzheimer's disease? Mom had a lot of those behaviors."

"Oh, it started 'bout a year ago. She's had a whole battery of tests. They think it's senile depression. Some of the behavior in this kind of depression is a lot like Alzheimer's disease, much like what your mother went through."

"That's too bad," Ben said. "Do you have children, Mr. Phillips?"

"No. My wife had a niece. She was real close to her, but the poor girl died. Soon after that, this all started."

"I know she must miss her," said Ben.

"I don't know, Sheriff," Mr. Phillips sighed. "Most of the time my wife don't make no sense. She's been so apprehensive watching the police out there. Everything sets her off. My greatest fear," he said, "to be perfectly frank, is suicide. They've told me that she might try it."

Matt could feel Jesse Phillips' pain. All the sorrow, anger, grief and helplessness that he had felt while caring for his mother surfaced. He wanted to reach out, to reassure and console his neighbor. Sensing his anguish, Ben continued quickly.

"Well, Mr. Phillips, tell you what, let me go on now and see what I can find out from other sources, and I'll be back if I feel it's really necessary to talk to your wife. The main thing I need now is to find either Mr. Hayes or some relative of Autumn Hayes. It appears that our investigation is more urgent than we first thought. We have found evidence that suggests that Autumn Hayes was murdered."

Jesse Phillips gawked at Ben.

Ben stood up, terminating the interview. "Have any idea where Hayes came from?" Ben asked as he moved toward the door.

Jesse Phillips regained his composure. "I believe I heard him say he worked for Computech. Autumn worked there, too. It's a company outside DC, in the Arlington area, if I remember correctly," Phillips said.

Matt said, "Yes, we knew that. That's where I cut my teeth twenty-some years ago. A good company."

Phillips stammered, "That's right. Forgot you were from Virginia, Matt. I remember now."

"Well, thanks Mr. Phillips," Ben said. The men stepped into the hall just as the gospel quartet began to encore their anthem, "Hope is an anchor...."

Matt glimpsed the bent figure of a rumpled, gray-haired woman, rocking back and forth. Tears stained her cheeks. It was so painful for Matt to see this familiar scene again. He pushed past Ben and into the cold air.

Ben grumbled as he descended the icy steps. "I don't like this one bit...not one damned bit."

"What do you mean?" asked Matt.

"Your neighbors. There's too many people who don't want to talk to me, who would be upset by my questioning them. No husband, no family, nobody knows them, nobody knows nothing about nothing. Something ain't right here, Matt."

CHAPTER 10

Matt returned home. The long walk back up the hill provided him with time to think. Old feelings and anxieties had been aroused. Suddenly, he felt a loss of control over his life again. That damned dream! By the time he reached his house, he was consumed by the calamity that had befallen this peaceful community.

Shoveling snow from the drive would provide the perfect diversion. By late afternoon, Matt viewed the cleared driveway with a feeling of accomplishment, and he realized for the first time how very hungry he was.

As he placed two large cans of chunky beef stew on the stove, Matt reached for the cordless and dialed Ignatius' number. As he stirred the stew and pushed the impatient cats from the kitchen counter, Matt reported the interviews with Jeffreys and Phillips to his friend.

"You didn't say anything about..." Ignatius began.

"No, I didn't mention the dream, and I'm not going to. I don't feel he needs that knowledge in order to generate suspicion. I agree with Ben. There are already too many unanswered questions. I don't like this, Nate. Not one bit."

"I agree. Gonna work tomorrow?"

"I sure hope so."

"Keep me informed."

"Right."

Matt clicked the off button. The two cats jumped back onto the counter as their cook reached for two large bowls. After filling the bowls, Matt set one on the table, and one on the floor. The cats sniffed the stew and shook their heads as steam arose from their bowl. Matt began to eat his supper heartily, watching amusedly as the cats inserted their paws, jerked them out quickly, and then licked the scrumptious stew from their pads.

Matt did not want to dream. The dream is what had forced his participation in this wretched escapade. Each time he began to dream, he would rouse himself to wakefulness. Finally, when his digital showed 6:00, Matt swung out of bed. An early breakfast and a pot of coffee would prime him for what he hoped would be a busy work day. A glance outside assured him that the storm had abated for the time being. Surely, the people at Langley would be able to reach their workplace this Friday morning and mercifully supply him with data to continue his research.

By 8:05, he had fed himself and the cats, shaved, and emerged from a steaming shower when the phone sounded. It would be 9:05 in Hampton. Perhaps a phone call would precede faxed data. Wrapping a towel around his waist, Matt dashed for the phone.

"Murray here."

"And Day here. How you doing, Matthew?"

"Cold and wet. I was in the shower."

"Sorry, pal. Just thought I'd bring you up to date on the Hayes case." Matt smiled.

"I need to ask you another small favor," Ben went on.

"Well, let's hear the update," Matt said. "And how small a favor?"

"Update first. You wanta do the good news/bad news thing?"

"Yeah, why not?"

"Well, the good news is I have some information on Autumn Hayes. While I was talking to your neighbors yesterday, Penny was getting one phone call after another from friends of Autumn Hayes. They are distraught. She'd never heard such crying and carrying on. Real pitiful, Penny said." He paused as if to allow a moment of silence before continuing. "They were inquiring about the arrangements. She had to tell them that arrangements were incomplete because we had not been able to locate any family. At any rate, Penny learned that Autumn belonged to Lakeside Tennis Club, the local country club, and some sailing group. She said she'd never heard such stirring testimonials to a young woman in her life. That little ol' gal must have spent a lot of time helping other people. Her friends said that she always seemed to be so happy and enthusiastic, the life-of-the party type. She was the first person her friends turned to when they had a problem or needed a confidant. It's a mystery to me how someone so well liked could end up murdered like this?"

"I don't know, Ben. This is really strange."

"Now for the bad news. In spite of having so many friends, would you believe nobody has any idea where J. R. Hayes could be? And *nobody* knows anything about her family or even where she comes from."

"That's incredible. Nobody even knows where the girl lived or where her family lives?"

"This is starting to smell like a day-old fish," Ben muttered.

"The favor?"

"Remember you told me yesterday that you used to work for Computech up in Virginia."

"Yeah, but that was a long time ago. Over 20 years ago."

"Well, do you still know anybody up there? Anybody who might have known the Hayeses or could get us information on them?"

Matt paused pensively. His mind switched back 20 years. "Oh, yes. I think I might know of someone. Caryn Shipley. She's an electrical engineer and worked in computer design. The last I heard she tracked into management."

"Great. She might be just the break we need to give us personal information on the Hayeses. When can you get in touch with her?"

"I'm not sure." Matt was a little taken aback. "I'm just assuming that she's still there. But I'll try this morning."

"Okay. Thanks. I'll wait to hear back from you."

"Okay, Ben. So long."

"So long, Matthew."

Matt pushed the off button. Would this never end? Each time he thought he was no longer involved in the Hayes ordeal, he got sucked back in. Pulling on jeans and a sweatshirt, he walked barefoot down the hall and into his study. A check of his fax showed no data. Well, he might as well get this inquiry over with. Reaching for the desk phone, he was amazed that he still remembered the central number of his first job place. He dialed. A voice confirmed his good memory. "Computech."

"Yes, I'd like to speak to Caryn Shipley."

"Ms. Shipley's extension is 2911 for your future reference. I'll ring, sir."

Several rings sounded.

"Ms. Shipley's office."

"May I speak to Ms. Shipley?"

"Who may I say is calling, please?"

"Tell her it's Matt Murray."

There was a pause. "Just a minute please, Mr. Murray."

A click preceded a soft, throaty voice with that Tidewater accent Matt knew so well.

"Matt Murray! Where in the world have you been all these years?"

CHAPTER 11

Years rolled away.

Caryn was memories. Sweet memories. She was memories of long, white arms and legs stretching out of sleeveless cotton dresses. She was sandled feet with pink toenails pumping a bicycle down a hot, dusty country road. She was the ocean breeze that caressed Matt's face as the Ferris wheel made its downward turn. She was an oval-shaped porcelain face set with jade eyes, framed with soft honey hair. And she had been engaged to Matt's best friend.

"Caryn. It's good to hear your voice."

"Matt Murray," she repeated, "you're the last person I would have expected to hear from today. Could this mean you're thinking about giving Computech another chance?"

"No, afraid not. I enjoy being my own boss too much."

"Well, then could this perhaps be *personal*?" The last word was little more than a hoarse whisper.

Matt laughed. "Now I remember why I spent my college years keeping you out of trouble. You're the only woman I know who can entice a man who is eight hundred miles away and snowed in under seven inches of snow."

"Well, Matt Murray, if it were your job to keep me out of trouble in Charlottesville, you surely screwed up. I suppose you've heard that Hank and I are divorced."

"Yes Caryn, I'm sorry."

"No need. I think we both knew it was no good. You know I never used his last name."

"Yes, but lots of women keep their own last name now."

"Lots of women didn't twenty-five years ago. We were too much alike. Besides, he wanted to work in California. I hadn't lost anything in California, and my job was important to me, too. So Hank joined the engineering exodus to California, and I made a place for myself here at Computech. I've no regrets. Not that there was ever much of a marriage anyway... not like you and Jill." She stopped suddenly. "By the way, Matt," her voice cracked, "I'm so sorry about Jill. I can never--"

"Thanks, Caryn." Matt interrupted in an effort to avoid the anguish that was always resurrected by memories of Jill. "She knew you cared. She knew we all did....But hey, this is about business." He made an effort to return the conversation to a less somber mood. "I understand that you tracked into management a few years ago, and I need to ask you about a former employee of Computech."

"Sure, Matt," Caryn was relieved to change the subject. "Be glad to help if I can. Who are we talking about?"

"Autumn Hayes. Her husband is James Hayes. He worked for Computech., also. I don't know what her maiden name was."

71

There was a momentary silence, followed by a nervous laugh. "If you're still in the business of keeping foolish young girls out of trouble, be aware that you might just be out of your league here. Autumn Hayes. Whew...that's a name I hadn't hoped to hear again."

"Come on, Caryn. You've really got my curiosity up now."

There was a long pause.

"Are you concerned about giving out information on former employees?" Matt pressed.

"Why do you need information on Autumn Hayes?" Caryn asked suspiciously.

"Autumn Hayes is dead, Caryn. The Sheriff is trying to locate her next of kin. James Hayes is apparently away on business and cannot be reached, and no one here seems to know anything about her family. Since she used to work for Computech, I was asked to make some inquiries."

"You're in law enforcement now?"

"No, damn it. Ben, the Sheriff, is a personal friend of mine. If this is going to cause a problem for you at work, forget it. I'll have Ben call officially."

"Don't be foolish, Matt. Of course I'll help. Autumn dead? Well, I can't say that I'm shocked, but I am sorry. Listen, let me go back and pull her record and make a few anecdotal notes. Also, I have an engineer here now who is from North Carolina, where she was from, and I'll see if he'll give you some information. He knew her before she came to work for us. I'll get all of this together, take it home tonight, slip into something interesting, pour myself a gin and tonic, and give you a call. How does that sound?"

"Twist of lime?"

"Yeah, twist of lime."

"It's a date. A long-distance date. Which is about the only kind of date I have with dangerous women like you."

"Matt, you do say the most lascivious things."

"Good-bye, Caryn."

"Bye, Matt." The rasping farewell was obviously exaggerated.

Matt smiled and shook his head as he pressed the off button. Caryn hadn't changed in twenty-some-odd years, since she introduced him to Jill that hot August night at Nags Head, North Carolina. They were at the Casino Dance Land, Mile Post 13. The clangor of the slot machines competed with the explosion of music from the band. Conversation had been impossible. For a while, it appeared that the relationship would not develop beyond a mere introduction. He remembered how Caryn had quickly led them off to the dunes, confident that the magic of the moonlight on the ocean would bewitch the two hopeless romantics. And it did.

Matt's return to the present was prompted by the receipt of a fax from Langley. The heat transfer data on the XA4B configuration had been reduced and was available on the Langley Cray YMP. He logged into the Langley computer through his modem and downloaded the data file. The afternoon was spent plotting the data on his workstation screen and comparing it with numerical predictions.

It had worked. Matt had actually enjoyed a full afternoon absorbed in his work and free from any thoughts of the "Hayes Case". As he stretched his arms to relieve his smarting muscles he thought, "Now for my date with Caryn."

CHAPTER 12

Matt was amazed to realize how much he anticipated the call from Caryn. Supper had been a hastily prepared tuna salad for him, plain tuna for Aslan and Spencer. He rinsed the dishes and loaded the dishwasher. As he watched the two cats clean their faces and paws, he began to consider what he'd have to drink during this long-distance rendezvous. Jack Daniels? Definitely, no. A brandy? Scotch? Now, where did he put that Chivas Regal? Matt moved sticky, dusty liquor bottles about on the top shelf of the kitchen cabinet. The unopened bottle was located. Next, he recovered one of Jill's fine Fostoria crystal snifters from the china closet. Matt dusted both bottle and snifter. Then, he placed the bottle and glass, a can of Planter's mixed nuts, and a paper towel onto a metal tray that had previously been used for backyard barbecues.

As he clattered down the hall to his office, he whistled a tune reminiscent of those bitter-sweet days. Yeah, those were the days when ideals were challenged and bruised, the days when youths were aroused and betrayed. Matt placed the tray on a small table beside the recliner. Then he positioned the telephone, a writing pad, and a pen next to the tray.

He sank into the softness of the leather cushion, extended his hands behind his head, and kicked back to wait for the telephone to ring. Those were the days, all right. Riotous times. Values being tried. A tool that had been designed to entertain and inform brought a kind of savagery into homes that had never before been imagined. Young men died before the viewer's eyes in some jungle thousands of miles away. A civil rights leader, a senator, and even a president were killed as viewers watched in horror. Each event that transpired produced an antithesis. The country had moved from flower power to acid rock. As Tiny Tim tiptoed through the tulips, Martin Luther King marched in Selma, Alabama. As Cassius Clay became Mohammed Ali, Timothy Leary "turned on, tuned in, and dropped out". Civil Rights marchers headed for Washington D. C., and hippies made their way to Woodstock, New York. Many young men and women chose to join the Peace Corps above the shouts of "burn, baby, burn!" that were coming out of such improbable places as Watts, Detroit, and My Lai. And, of course, the big question that all American youth sought to answer was "What the hell is a Spiro Agnew?" Matt emitted a soft laugh and lifted the snifter to his nose. He laid his head back and allowed the warm liquid to trickle down his throat. Yes, those were the days.

Matt disliked confrontation. He damned near ran from it. It was too easy for him to understand everyone's point of view. That's why he had become an engineer. Engineering was absolute, no gray areas. He avoided long tedious debates concerning controversial political issues and eroding social values. When the pressure to become involved became too great, Matt would escape to the Outer Banks...Jockey Ridge, Nags Head, Manteo, Kitty Hawk, Ocracoke, Hatteras. The phenomenon of the storm-swept Outer Banks was that, in spite of the shifting shoreline, other things appeared to remain the same there...the ocean, the dunes, the people. He could almost smell the brackish air inundating a fishing pier and feel the warmth of the sand beneath his bare feet. He could feel the skin on his face tighten from the blistering sun. He could swear that he heard the screech of sea gulls above lapping waves. Squawk, squawk, squawk. Ring, Ring, Ring.

"Hello. Murray."

"Matt," the voice whispered, "It's Caryn."

"Ah, yes, Caryn. My but you are beautiful tonight."

"Now how do you know that?"

"Because you always look beautiful. Did you know that in college your nickname was Caryn Shapely...not Shipley?"

"Yes, I knew that. What a memory you have."

"Contacting you brought back so much that I'd forgotten. You know...the beach, the University, all those crazy, wonderful times." Matt paused, "Hey, I almost forgot why I called you. Behave yourself, now."

"Me? Behave myself? I'm just dutifully following your instructions."

"Yeah, right. Does that mean you have some information for me on Autumn Hayes?"

"Sure do. Lots. How do you want it? From the shrink, from her employer, or from the guy next door? I got it all."

"Why don't you just give it to me however you feel most comfortable?"

"Right. Well I'll start with her job at Computech. Autumn Hayes came to work here five years ago this month. Her maiden name was Reynolds. She came here from Raleigh, North Carolina where she attended Our Capital's Business College. She took a two-year course.

77

Let's see, she took typing, shorthand, accounting, computer technology, computer lab..."

"Forget that, Caryn. Go on to when she is at Computech."

"Okay. Well, she was placed in my division in design. She was a good worker, Matt. She trained so easily. She was the first one here in the morning, and the last one to leave at night. She obviously had good training, and she also mastered new skills very quickly. I thought I'd found a jewel. Pretty soon she was helping others who had been here much longer than she. That's when I started noticing her interaction with other people. At first, I thought she merely exhibited strong leadership qualities. She was so well liked that the others in the office competed for her acceptance. Then I realized that it went beyond that. She had an unusual ability to control. I wasn't concerned as long as this didn't create problems, but it eventually did.

"Autumn had been able to avoid suspicion because of her good front. She had a great sense of humor. She always had a little joke she wanted to whisper privately to some individual...usually a man. She had an exaggerated sense of self-worth of which she constantly reminded everyone. She told some grandiose tales. I remember that she enjoyed talking about a study she'd read that showed that left-handed people are more imaginative. She attached sexual significance to that creativity and imagination. Autumn, of course, was left-handed. I have no idea if such a study existed.

"She appeared, however, to be optimistic and encouraging to others. She was charming and likable and had a disarming smile. She exuded sincerity and openness. I watched her often as some fellow worker confided a problem to her. She was a master at showing concern and understanding...the old eye contact thing as someone poured out their innermost pain, an occasional look of shock and disbelief, and even upon occasion, a tear or two. She had very good insight into the needs and weaknesses of people. Unfortunately, by the time one realized how devious she was, she had inflicted a lot of hurt. To hear her talk, however, you'd think that she was an eminently moral person."

There was a pause as Caryn collected her thoughts. Matt said, "I suppose this eventually caused problems on the job."

"Yes it did." Caryn continued, "I watched with alarm as Autumn became more and more accomplished at manipulating her co-workers. Since I was detached from the regular office work force, I was able to discern things that the more involved staff members could not. Autumn appeared to use her insight into the needs of others to control and exploit them. It was like a game to her. The exploitations took the form of everything from social popularity to on-the-job evaluations and raises. She seemed devoid of guilt when she victimized someone. Instead of feeling sorry for those she hurt, she would show absolute contempt for them. It seemed that she could, in fact, find ways to project blame onto the victim of the very misfortune she had arranged. I also soon learned that she was a chronic liar. If caught in a lie, she would promise to make amends, but never intending to do so. Although she was great at making friends, she couldn't keep them very long. She seemed to think that she deserved the utmost consideration and accepted no blame for anything, even if her deviousness was exposed beyond a doubt."

"This must have been difficult for you," Matt sympathized.

"It got worse." Caryn explained, "I soon recognized another trait which would prove to be most alarming. Autumn was quite a thrill-seeker. She liked skydiving, white-water rafting, hang gliding, and claimed to have tried bullfighting in Mexico, which I didn't believe. And I soon realized that the thrills extended to personal relationships too. It seemed that the more stable a marriage appeared to be, the more of a challenge that was to Autumn. Pretty soon I'd notice private jokes and lustful glances between her and her current conquest. The affair would rage on for several weeks with a callous disregard for the feelings of the unsuspecting wife. Then when the innocent spouse was completely shattered, Autumn was able to convince people that she was not only free of fault, but that the wife was responsible for the whole affair. She blamed the victim. And people bought it. They always bought it, at least for a while."

"How did this affect her job performance?" Matt asked.

Matt heard the click of ice against glass. After a brief pause, Caryn continued, "Autumn did her work skillfully and accurately, however, the work of others in the office was profoundly affected. I began to think that the efficient section I'd worked so hard to put together was in real jeopardy. It's alarming to think that one person can be so destructive. I came to the conclusion that I had to get rid of her. I had set up a meeting with the company psychiatrist to get some help in dealing with her kind of personality. I don't mind telling you, I felt inept when it came to dealing with the likes of Autumn Hayes. But as fate would have it, the meeting with Dr. Harding was unnecessary.

"Autumn's next pursuit was of a young man--" Matt could hear paper rattling. "Joseph Dixson. Joseph and his wife had been married three or four years. They had been desperately trying to have children. If I remember correctly, there were several miscarriages. Anyway, Joe was very protective of his wife. She was constantly battling depression. I never will forget the day I looked through the glass wall of my office into the outer office. There were Joe and Autumn, heads close together, whispering. Autumn was using that intense eye contact thing that seemed to bore into the very soul of her latest prey. She applied her sincerest looks of pity and understanding. That was one of the times she managed a tear or two. I remember thinking, 'Don't do it, Joe, don't fall for it', but of course he did. Autumn found numerous ways to "help" Joe with his work. There were the inside jokes and the looks. Once, I confronted them about taking too long for lunch, and I could swear that I heard snickering as I walked away. They behaved like high school kids. I don't know how all this got back to his wife, but much later I was told there was an anonymous phone call. At any rate, Joe didn't show up for work one day. Autumn was in a dither. She expressed alarm to anyone who would listen. She even had a programmer call Joe's house. No answer."

Caryn hesitated and sighed audibly. She continued, "About noon, I received a call from Joe's mother. She was at the hospital. Joe's wife had just died from an overdose of the medication she'd been taking for depression. I called a meeting to inform the staff. You should have seen the dramatic act that Autumn performed. Well, I won't go into that. Over the next few days, Autumn waged a campaign to portray the deceased as a villain. How dare she put Joe through this, etc., etc. Somehow it didn't take this time. I think the whole episode was so damned tragic that everyone was shocked into the realization of just what Autumn was capable of doing. And what she'd done here was just short of murder. But this is not the end of the story. When poor old Joe came back to work, she was there, tears streaming down her cheeks, whispers of condolences, and an invitation to lunch. And what did Joe do to repay Autumn for her kindness, her friendship, her concern? He gave Autumn his wife's beloved pet, a little dog. It was a white toy poodle, and it had been his wife's child substitute. Talk about a tragedy.

"Just when the office was about to erupt with indignation, Autumn walked into my office and said, 'Guess what? I'm getting married, to James Hayes...you know, over in testing'. I didn't know whether to laugh or cry. But I certainly did feel relieved. She left quietly. There were none of the parties or fanfare usually given a bride-to-be or a person leaving the company."

"I'm sure you felt relieved." Matt said.

"Relief is putting it mildly." Caryn replied. "I no longer had an official reason to confer with Dr. Harding, but I was so affected by Autumn that I collected my notes and kept the appointment. The information I gave him was basically what I've told you. Although Dr. Harding did not have the opportunity to interview Autumn personally, he suggested that the behavior I described was characteristic of a sociopath. These people are often very bright, but have not developed morally or ethically according to society's standards. They are thrill-seekers who live for the moment with no regard for the rights or well-being of the people around them. He added that he probably would not have been able to help Autumn, as traditional methods of intervention have not proven to be successful in changing these people's behavior

"So, that is the story of Autumn Reynolds Hayes at Computech. What do you think of your neighbor now?"

Matt sat back and sighed. "I had no idea. Caryn that must have been hell!"

"Right. That was my first encounter with this kind of person, and I hope my last. I did learn a lot, though. When Autumn came to work for me, she was so bright and skillful and eager to learn. I thought she was too good to be true. And she was."

"You sound a little cynical, too."

"Yes, I suppose. Now, you want to hear about *the kid next door*?"

"You mean there's more?"

"Oh, yes, there's more. The information may not be so pertinent, but it is insightful."

"Sure. Let's have it." Matt flipped the page of his writing pad and reached for his glass.

"I talked with one of Autumn's co-workers, Brian Axelrod. Brian is a young engineer who works in another section of Computech. He came to work here several weeks before Autumn served up her resignation. I was in the cafeteria when he first bumped into her at work. He obviously knew her. He appeared to be delighted. She appeared to be abashed. I remember how she rushed out without going through the lunch line.

"A few weeks later, I sought out Brian in an effort to have as much information as I could about Autumn before I kept my appointment with Dr. Harding. Brian was most willing to talk with me and answered any questions I had. So I'm sure he would be glad to talk with your friend, the Sheriff. Here...let me give you his home address and phone number."

Matt wrote down the number Caryn read to him. When he looked at the clock, Matt realized they had talked for over an hour. Although the topic of conversation had been an unpleasant one, the visit with Caryn had been delightful. The silence at the other end of the phone told Matt that she too was reluctant to end the tryst. He laid the writing pad and pen on the table and cleared his throat.

"Caryn, what can I say? It's been great...regardless."

"Yes, great," she whispered. "Call me again sometime?"

"Sure."

"About something more *alluring*."

"Behave yourself now...yes, about something more *alluring*," Matt mimicked.

"Good night, Matt."

"Night, Caryn."

As Matt pressed the off button, the house suddenly seemed still, empty, almost deserted. He laid his head back and listened as the wind wailed through the barren trees.

CHAPTER 13

Saturday Morning

Ben sat behind his cluttered desk and stared at a scrap of paper on which was written Brian Azelrod's address and telephone number. Then, lifting a pen, he scribbled questions on a pad to ask about Autumn Hayes. Finally, he tossed the wrinkled slip of paper across the desk.

"Penny, how about getting me Mr. Brain Axelrod up in Virginia on the telephone?"

The rhythmic click of the word processor came to an abrupt halt. A head, tousled with brilliant copper curls turned to face Ben. Almond-shaped eyes, made larger by thick layers of shadow and mascara, glared at him. The pouting, red lips mouthed a single, indistinguishable expletive. Penny heaved her chair away from her desk, and with an audible sigh, she rose and strutted across the room. She sported tight, faded jeans and leather high-heel boots. Her over-sized red turtleneck sweater was unable to conceal the ample bosom of the otherwise petite young woman. Penny jerked up the message on which was written the phone number and stared at it impatiently. She snatched the phone on Ben's desk and brutally punched the eleven numbers.

Penny smacked her gum and counted the rings. Just as she decided to hang up, a sleepy voice said, "Hello."

"Mr. Brian Axelrod, please. Sheriff Benjamin Day calling from Winchester, Tennessee."

"Yes...this is Brian Axelrod."

"Just a minute, please." Penny shoved the receiver in Ben's direction. "Here!" She retreated to her desk.

"Mr. Axelrod, this here is Benjamin Day, Sheriff of Franklin County, Tennessee. We've had a most unfortunate incident to take place in our community. I'm sorry to tell you that a friend of yours, Miz Autumn Hayes, has been found dead. Since Miz Hayes' death was not due to natural causes, it's necessary to conduct an investigation. Ms. Caryn Shipley, a former employer of Miz Hayes, provided me with your name as one who may have some information on the deceased."

"Yes. Caryn told me about Autumn's death. She said you might call. I knew Autumn for a long time. Haven't seen her in over a year, though." The voice was no longer sleepy.

"I see. Would you mind answering a few questions?"

"No. Certainly not."

"First off, Mr. Axelrod...do you have any idea where I could find James Hayes, her husband?"

"No...not at all. I don't know him. Just Autumn."

"I see. Well, Mr. Axelrod, Ms. Shipley told us that when Autumn Hayes ran into you there at Computech, she didn't appear to be interested in renewing your acquaintance."

Brian explained that he wasn't surprised at Autumn's cool reception. He claimed he was familiar with her erratic behavior. He had been a neighbor of Autumn Reynolds in their childhood. He began, "You see Autumn and her sister, Spring--"

"Spring?" Ben interrupted.

"Yes, there were only a few months' difference in their ages. Autumn was born in the fall and Spring..."

"Let me guess...was born in the Spring."

"Yes. End of August and end of June, if I remember correctly."

"Tell you what, Mr. Axelrod," Ben said, "Why don't you just give me the whole story of her background as you know it. Then, if I have any questions, I'll ask."

"Well, okay." Ben could hear a rustle, and he envisioned Brian moving to a comfortable position. "The girls were raised by their grandmother in Randolph County, North Carolina. It's basically a farming area, a few miles from Greensboro. Their grandmother was the county character. Her appearance was bizarre and her behavior eccentric. Consequently, she was featured as the main character in some very colorful local stories.

"I remember that her looks fascinated us kids. She had faded red hair all streaked with white, and she used a bunch of oily, dirty combs to pile her matted hair on top of her head. Her skin was yellow, and she sucked constantly on an unfiltered cigarette. She did this trick that really fascinated us. She'd allow the smoke to curl slowly up into her nose. There was a faint outline of a mustache that was made darker by the tobacco stains. She was a heavy woman, and wheezed when she walked. She wore old wrinkled dresses that reached all the way down to her ankles, and she cinched a cowboy belt around her waist.

"We boys were particularly taken with her because she always had a 'naughty little joke' to tell. She was apparently an alcoholic, and she delighted in being the one to give a kid his first drink. She called it their initiation into manhood, and she'd laugh and jiggle while the kid sputtered and coughed.

"Grand, as she liked to be called, owned a small country store with one gas pump outside and a grill inside. She sold fishing and hunting licenses, gasoline, junk food, and beer. So the place was always full of farmers, hunters, and little kids."

Brian sighed and paused in his recollections.

Ben said, "Did the girls always live with their grandmother?"

"Oh, no," said Brian. "As a matter of fact, I'll never forget the night Autumn and Spring came to live with Grand. I was there at the store with my Pop, who was enjoying his weekly game of pool. I was sitting on a stool at the grill counter, nursing a soda and watching my Dad.

"We heard the blast of a car horn and the sound of country music from a car radio. Grand pushed herself up and wobbled to the screen door.

"My kid's curiosity got the best of me, so I peeped out of the door. Outside, a battle raged. It went on for quite some time. Grand waved her arms and swore while a tall thin woman puffed on a cigarette and blew smoke in Grand's direction. The car had a Fort Bragg sticker on its bumper, and a soldier sat inside, completely detached from the fight. Finally, the skinny woman dropped the cigarette and crushed it.

"She turned abruptly, opened the back door, and reached into the car. From inside the car she yanked a skinny, stringy-haired, shoeless little girl. Tumbling out behind this kid was her duplicate, except the second girl was smaller than the first. The first little girl had a defiant look that she flashed from one woman to the other. The second child whimpered and moved closer to the larger child. The woman jumped back into the car. Tires squealed, and it disappeared into the night.

"So that's how Autumn and Spring came to live with Grand." Brian said. He paused and then continued. "They were four and five years old and could almost pass for twins. Spring was timid, quiet, almost withdrawn. Learning was hard for her, and she had a lot of trouble in school. She had difficulty making friends, and Autumn seemed to be her only playmate. That suited Autumn just fine. Autumn delighted in having control over her younger sister, and she was always the leader in any game. She was defiant, competitive, and appeared to be afraid of nothing. She and Grand would get into shouting matches sometimes, and poor Spring would just cringe in fear." Brian sighed pensively.

Ben waited a few seconds, and then asked, "How did Grand treat the little girls?"

"Grand's parenting skills were unorthodox, to say the least." Brian explained. "Her idea of quality time was to crowd the girls and any other kids who wanted to go into the back of her old beat-up pickup truck. Then, under the cover of darkness, we'd bounce along on the country roads searching for 'the mischief' as Grand would say. We'd find a watermelon patch or a field of ripe corn, and Grand would say, 'Go to it, you little raccoons'. This thievery went on for several summers. Then Grand got too greedy. She thought it would be a good idea to sell some of the corn we'd picked during our nighttime raids. When a basket full of fresh corn appeared outside the store with a big For Sale sign stuck in the basket, folks let Grand know she'd gone too far this time. It was a long time before kids were allowed to go back to the store. But Grand just laughed and vowed they'd get over it. They did."

Brian hesitated as he struggled with less pleasant memories. "Grand had a temper, and consequently, the girls suffered some harsh punishments. I remember one day when Grand was polishing the stove, Autumn and Spring walked into the store to find as much black stove polish on Grand's face as was on the stove. The girls and the rest of us kids couldn't help but laugh at the sight of Grand on her knees, rear projected upward, polishing away on her beloved pot-belly. Grand, however, failed to see the humor in the situation. She grabbed the girls by their arms, dragged them into the back room, and locked them in a dark storage closet. The rest of us scattered. The girls never protested this kind of punishment. They knew it would just make matters worse. This time, Grand actually forgot them. About nine o'clock that evening, one of the customer asked where they were. Grand threw her hands up in the air and shouted, 'Oh, my Lord!' When she opened the door to the dark closet, the two girls were huddled in a corner. Autumn was cradling Spring in her arms and softly singing, "Put your arms around me, honey, hold me tight." It was a pitiful sight, and I remember feeling so sorry for them."

Brian wavered as he recalled the pitiful scene. Ben waited patiently, and then asked a less intense question, "Were the girls good students?"

"Autumn was real bright in school." Brian replied. "She was the first one in class to catch on to a new kind of math problem. Her report card was always straight A's, and she let everyone know it. She certainly wasn't a teacher-pleasing student, however. Autumn was always at the bottom of any classroom conflict, but she was seldom found out and almost never punished. She was a cheerleader, member of the Beta Club, and captain of the debating team. She was also the valedictorian of her graduating class.

"After graduation from high school, Autumn announced that she was going to business college. She chose Our Capitol's Business College in Raleigh, North Carolina. No one knew where she got the money, and no one asked. Grand voiced no objection or interest. Her attitude was almost one of easy come, easy go. However, the separation of the girls was traumatic for Spring. I went with them that Sunday morning as the two girls walked arm in arm down to the main highway. Autumn carried only one suitcase. Spring cried as they waited by the road for the local bus. They flagged the bus down, and Autumn climbed aboard. She ran to the back window. I remember how the two girls waved to each other until the bus disappeared. When Autumn left, Spring went into deep depression. We all felt sorry for her, but being kids, we didn't know how to bring her out of it. I didn't see her much after that because I left for college myself. I went to North Carolina State University, which is also in Raleigh. I ran into Autumn occasionally. The business college is right down Hillsboro

Street from the University. However, Autumn made it clear that she had no desire to reestablish a friendship with me. I guessed she wanted to put her past behind her, and I couldn't blame her. Eventually, I completely lost track of her. I wasn't surprised, however, to learn that she'd gone to work for Computech. I always felt she'd make good...one way or the other." His last words were hardly audible.

Brian cleared his throat. "So, that's the story of little Autumn Reynolds Hayes. I don't know if the childhood is very relevant to your investigation, but it does explain some of her behavior...in a sad sort of way," Brian concluded.

"Do I detect a hint of pity for Autumn Hayes?" asked Ben.

"Well, yes...for the Autumn Reynolds who was dumped at Grand's store in Randolph County, North Carolina, when she was five years old," Brian clarified. "Any questions I can answer, Sheriff?"

"Lemme see." Ben collected his thoughts. "Do you know if Autumn went back to Grand's after she went away to college?"

"Not that I know of. Autumn would have been short of money, and she didn't have a car. In fact, she didn't drive."

"Whatever happened to Grand?"

"Grand died about four or five years ago. She was found in her store by a couple of kids. She had a massive stroke. Neither of the girls attended her funeral."

"I bet that caused a lot of talk."

"No," Brian said. "No one really expected them to ever come back, not even to her funeral."

"Yeah. I think I can understand that myself. What about Spring?"

"She left, too. I came home for N.C. State University one holiday and learned she'd gone. No one knew where."

"And the mother?"

"Oh, I don't even know her name. Just know that folks were careful not to mention her in the presence of Grand. Even Autumn and Spring never talked about her. As far as I know, she hasn't been to Randolph County since dropping off the girls that night. Sorry, I can't help you on the next-of-kin thing."

"Well, Mr. Axelrod. I thank you for your time," concluded Ben. "And if you should think of anything at all that could help me out, I'd sure appreciate hearing from you."

"Of course, Sheriff. Good-bye."

"Good-bye, Mr. Axelrod." Ben dropped the receiver into its cradle and stared at the near-blank note pad. He'd hoped to fill it with relevant information that would help him solve the murder of Autumn Hayes.

CHAPTER 14

It was 4:30 p.m. Ben had spent the entire Monday in court. As he left the second floor courtroom, he peered anxiously out of the window as the foreboding snow continued its slow descent from the darkening sky. Quickly he moved down the stone steps to the main floor of the courthouse.

From his early childhood, the courthouse had been fascinating to Ben. Gracing the walls of the hallway by the south entrance were murals that depicted life in Franklin County from the earliest settlers in 1700 to the rebuilding of a war-ravaged South. As a boy, Ben had felt a special affinity with one character in the mural; a Native American crouched upon a mountain overlooking the bustling frontier community that would become Winchester, Tennessee. Ben had tried to imagine how the watcher felt as he observed the settlers clear his hunting grounds and build a town molded to meet the needs of the white man. Had he felt fear? Anger? Curiosity?

Inlaid in the marble floor of the main corridor was a large terrazzo map of Franklin County. Different colors of stone designated towns and significant sites of the area and indicated the perimeter of the county. Young Ben had made a game of skipping across this stone county. He'd slide down the mountain from Sewanee to Winchester or hop over to the town of Estill Springs. On a particularly adventurous day, five giant steps allowed the boy to journey down to the Alabama state line. There was little doubt in Ben's mind that this map game had helped him develop an accurate perception of the lay-out of the county.

A glance at his watch warned Ben that he would be late again. He quickened the pace. This was the night for dinner and a weekly game of pool at Ignatius Harder's place.

The courtroom had been hot, stuffy, and very crowded. Even the harsh weather had not deterred those spectators who regularly came to observe justice in action. Ben's head hurt and his eyes burned. He walked swiftly past the bulletin board where scowling faces glared at him from wanted posters. Flyers declared a $1,000 reward for information leading to the arrest of anyone hunting wild turkey. The reward was increased to $3,000 for poachers.

As he opened the door and stepped outside, the first blasts of frigid air stung his nostrils and assaulted his lungs. He paused outside the courthouse to pull on his jacket and allow his body to adjust to the sudden change in temperature.

Ben descended the steps of the courthouse. Through the snow he could spot an illuminated marquee assuring parents that the movie currently being shown was rated PG. This scene was so tranquil and sanguine that Ben almost expected to see James Stewart racing around the square yelling, 'Merry Christmas, old theater. Merry Christmas, old pawn shop. Merry Christmas, old bank. Merry Christmas, Old Bedford Falls'. Ben smiled at the association.

His reverie was interrupted by the groan of an engine. Stepping into the street, Ben could see past the Masonic Lodge and down the hill of Dinah Shore Blvd., named for the town's most celebrated native. An old rusty salt truck complained noisily as it made its way up the hill. Close behind the old relic was an impatient Ford Escort. Unable to pass the truck, it gunned its motor relentlessly. Slowly, the two vehicles moved up the hill and into the square. The driver of the salt truck lifted a hand in Ben's direction. The driver of the car grinned and waved also. As the Ford passed, Ben noted a Minnesota license plate. A sticker on the bumper of the car proclaimed in large red letters, *"Sewanee ain't a river it's the University of the South"*.

"Hey, Sheriff! How you like this snow?" The shout came from a boy who was hanging out of the window of the passenger's side.

"Be careful going up that mountain," Ben warned.

"Right, Sheriff. See ya." The voice faded as the young man retreated into the car.

Ben enjoyed a good relationship with the University of the South Students and the high school kids. They had a healthy combination of respect and admiration for the Jolly Green Giant, a title considered appropriate for the big, amiable sheriff who sported a green uniform.

The Sheriff pointed his car in the direction of First Street, and he slowly moved past City Hall. The dark office windows testified that no one chose to work late tonight. Glancing to his right, he recognized a tan Cutlass Olds and its white-haired driver. Her arms stretched upward and her hands tightly grasped the steering wheel. Mrs. Ernestine, retired from teaching, was now the matriarchal owner of Golden Leaves Bookstore over on Second Ave NW. Her dedication as owner of the town's only bookstore dictated that the citizenry should always have access to a good book...especially on a snowy day. She released her tightly gripped fingers and wiggled them in a greeting to Ben, never once moving her eyes from the traffic light.

Ben approached the Trinity Episcopal Church, a small building of Country Gothic architectural style. The lonely light burning in the rector's office confirmed that service as well as age had earned respect for the small parish. Turning left onto Cedar Street, then Second Ave. SW, Ben finally stopped the patrol car in front of the Sheriff's Office.

Clouds of cigarette smoke assaulted Ben as he stepped into the glass-paneled office. A radio crackled in the background and the smell of popcorn competed with the smell of smoke. Penny sat behind a desk that was cluttered with scattered papers of different colors, ballpoint pens, paperclips, telephone, file baskets, framed pictures, an almost-dead plant, and an empty microwave popcorn bag. Penny's black sweatshirt was encrusted with studs, pieces of colored glass, and gold and red glitter. The brilliant hair that had earned her the name of Penny was moussed and spritzed into an outrageous do that twisted and swirled in all directions. She focused her heavily shadowed eyes on Ben and pointed a red acrylic nail at him.

"Sheriff, why don't you pick up your messages?"

"Been in court all day, Penny."

"Just look at all I have to do." She waved a hand above the cluttered desk. "I'm way behind in my work. I have to keep up with messages for all of you. I don't have any help. The phone rings constantly, mostly about Autumn Hayes. Sheriff, you're gonna have to decide what to do about her, you know. What am I suppose to tell them? Huh? Aren't you even gonna take them?"

Ben reached for the batch of messages written in Penny's neat, broad handwriting. He shuffled through the notes quickly, perusing each one. "Penny, the instructions haven't changed. Just tell them arrangements are incomplete until notification of next of kin. It's that simple. No kin, no arrangements. I'm on my way over to Ignatius Harder's place. Call me there if something important comes up. I gotta have some rest and down time." He stuffed the messages in his shirt pocket, smiled at Penny's pouting red lips, and walked out.

CHAPTER 15

As Ben ascended the icy ramp to Ignatius Harder's porch, he found that his hands were too frozen to grasp the handrail. He further realized that the iron knocker was covered by a thin sheet of ice, rendering it useless. A sound thud of his fist elicited a response from inside. The door flew open and the skinny, white dog, wrapped in a red towel this time, yelped incessantly as Matt motioned Ben into the house.

"Hey, Ignatius, it's Ben."

"Well, it's about time."

"Now don't you two start. I just got chewed up and spit out by Penny. I've been in court all day. I do have a job, you know. Since this Autumn Hayes mess, my life ain't been my own." As he talked, Ben removed his coat and hung it on an oak peg beside the door. He sniffed. The scent of unidentifiable spices mixed with the smell of chocolate, coffee, and wood burning in the fireplace. A gnawing feeling in his stomach reminded Ben that he had not eaten since breakfast. He walked into the kitchen.

"Say 'Natius, something sure smells good. Don't see how you come up with these delicious dishes."

Ignatius removed a foil cover from a large Pyrex dish and, using a wooden spoon, tasted its contents. "I enjoy cooking. Just follow directions, and it will turn out okay. No surprises. No disappointments. Just follow a neat, simple plan."

"Yeah, maybe for you," said Matt. "You underestimate your skill, Nate. Not everyone can just follow directions and come out with meals like yours."

"Say, what is this?" said Ben as he picked up a 3x5 index card covered with smudges. "Is this your directions, 'Natius?"

"Yeah, it's called a recipe, Ben," Ignatius said testily.

"Look at all the stuff that went into this." Ben counted aloud. "Fourteen ingredients. Can you believe that, Matt?"

"Sure can't," Matt replied. "I never cook anything that calls for more than four ingredients. I'm impressed, Nate."

"Yeah, well, that's why we eat here instead of at your place."

Ben examined a second card, equally as grimy as the first. "Mississippi Mud," he read. "So that's the scrumptious chocolate smell."

Ignatius paused in his culinary endeavors. "Let's eat first and skip all shop talk. Then, while we have coffee and dessert, you two can fill me in on the latest in the Autumn Hayes case. After that, we can concentrate on some serious pool. You guys are in to me for big stakes now. What is it? Ben.....25, and Matt you're approaching 10. Can't let you two leave owing me that kind of match sticks."

Having established the schedule for the evening, Pete led the way to the table. He went directly to Ignatius' chair, hunkered down, and waited with tongue extended. Ignatius reached for a small dish that was in his lap and filled it with a generous portion of the evening's entree.

"Chicken with artichoke hearts is going to be one of Pete's favorites. But just wait till you see him put away that Mississippi Mud. I won't give him much of that, though. Dogs aren't supposed to eat sweets, you know. Gives them worms."

He set Pete's dish on the floor. The dish was soon lapped clean. The animal seemed to inhale the contents.

Dinner conversation revolved around the winter storm. Meteorologists were now confirming that the area over which the current front was stalled included middle Tennessee. Matt complained about not getting data from Langley; Ben complained about the havoc created by the storm and the Autumn Hayes Case; and Ignatius just complained. The serenity of the moment was even appreciated by Pete. He moved to the fireplace, turned around three times, and lay down contentedly for the night.

The three men enjoyed their dessert and coffee as they sat in overstuffed chairs before a blazing fire. As Matt moved to refill their cups, Ignatius reached for his pipe and said, "Well, lemme hear the results of your sleuthing. What did you find out when you called Caryn?"

"Well, I found out a lot. I don't know how useful it will be to Ben in solving the Autumn Hayes murder, but I got a lot of background stuff." Matt collected his thoughts and revealed all the details of his conversation with Caryn.

Then Ben told about his telephone conversation with Brian Axelrod. When he concluded his report, the three men sat silently for a long time. Only the ticking of the clock and the moan of the wind interrupted the silence being observed in reverence to the drama they had just heard.

Matt broke the silence. "What kind of a mother would do a thing like that? Leave her kids in a situation where she knew how bad it was going to be. That's probably why she left herself. Then to bring those little girls back and dump them there, she oughta be--"

"A cowbird!" Ignatius boomed.

"What?" Both Matt and Ben gaped at Ignatius.

"What are you talking about?" asked Matt.

"A brown-headed cowbird. That's what the mother acted like." Ignatius picked up a copy of Peterson's field guide to bird identification and flipped to a certain page. "Here, read for yourself. The brown-headed cowbird gets pregnant, doesn't want to be tied down and take care of the chicks, so she lays her eggs in the nest of some other bird. The unsuspecting bird hatches and raises the little cowbird while the mother cowbird drives off with some soldier from Fort Bragg. See for yourself."

Matt lifted a palm to Ignatius. "I believe you, 'Nate. She does sound that irresponsible. That makes for a sad life for a little kid. But we have to remember that the kid grew -up and did some not-so-nice things herself."

"Well, I have to confess that I, for one, was starting to get pretty bored with all of Autumn Hayes' niceness," Ignatius said. "Anybody that *nice* is suspect. I can appreciate good, but deliver me from *nice*. In my opinion, now we've got ourselves a credible human being."

"Just listen to yourself," said Ben. "You'd think you admired that woman or something."

"I didn't say I admired the woman. I said she was more believable."

"Ignatius, the cynic," declared Matt.

"Well, you may call me a cynic, but I say it's being realistic. Poor ol' Pete. No telling what he went through. We should have known that it takes a vicious person to shave him like that. He was defenseless. Totally dependent."

"Hey, Nate, this is about Autumn Hayes, okay?" said Ben. "Matt, what do you suppose happened to Spring?"

Ignatius would have no part of it. "You know what galls me? It galls me that people like that can even have animals." The other two men gaped at him. "That's right. I think owning a pet should be a privilege, not a right. And then, when the abusive owner gets tired of the pet, or in this case dies, do you think the animal is placed with the person who can take the best care of him? Hell, no. Some judge or someone just says, 'It's property. It just goes to the next of kin.' No regard given to the animal's wishes or what's best for him." Ignatius paused abruptly and puffed on his pipe.

"'Natius, are you afraid someone is going to take Pete away?" Ben asked. "Hey buddy, chances are Hayes won't want Pete anyway. Hell, when the dog's first mistress died, her husband gave him to Autumn. I'll bet Hayes will be glad to find a home for Pete."

"Yeah, Nate," Matt interjected, "most single men don't want to be tied down with a pet."

Ben and Matt's attempts at reassurance were interrupted by the ring of the telephone. Ignatius lifted the receiver. "Awright...yeah...wait. Ben, it's for you."

Ben stood up and walked with the remote phone into the kitchen. Matt and Ignatius sat in awkward silence.

"More coffee?" Matt moved toward the pot.

"Yeah, thanks," mumbled Ignatius. He had let down his emotional guard and was relieved to have attention diverted from him.

Ben returned coat in hand to where his friends were sitting. "Gotta go. That was Penny. News from the State Highway Patrol. They found James Hayes' car on I-24 just this side of Murfreesboro. Single-car accident. It was in the ditch almost hidden in a snow bank. Inside, they found a body. Chest busted…several broken ribs, and some internal damage. 'Pears like the actual cause of death is that he froze. Name on the license identifies the driver as James R. Hayes of Winchester, Tennessee. This puts a whole new spin on things, guys. Up till now, James R. Hayes has been my number one suspect. Now I got to get off my butt and find another one." Ben had his coat on now. "Matt, this makes it real important for me to talk to all your neighbors now, especially the evasive ones. Could I ask you to accompany me again tomorrow morning when I interview them?"

"Sure, Ben, be glad to help. What time?"

"Let's not be too early. How about nine?"

"Fine. I'll meet you outside Ignatius' house."

Ben moved toward the door. "Thanks for another delicious supper, 'Natius. Now don't you worry about Pete, especially now." Turning to Matt he added, "We'll get our pool revenge next week, huh, Matthew?"

"Right, Ben."

The door closed, and Ben was gone. Matt and Ignatius sat in silence watching the flames leap and ignite a newly added log. The sparks popped and cracked as the fire cast long, eerie shadows on the wall.

"Ben's right, you know. I don't think you'll have to worry about keeping Pete now. Seems to me like Pete's an orphan."

"No, I don't suppose I have to worry now."

As if realizing that he was the topic of conversation, the dog arose, stretched, and then dropped back down upon his bed of red towels.

CHAPTER 16

Matt promised to call Ignatius with a full report of the interviews with the neighbors. He then proceeded to trek back up the hill to the security of his own hearth and home. Pushing his way headlong into the darkness, he noticed that light snow still wafted sluggishly in the night air, contributing to the existing burden on utility wires and tree branches. Matt hardly noticed the luminescence of his neighbor's windows. The light, so reassuring in the past, now did nothing to allay his apprehensions. He diverted his attention in the opposite direction as he walked pass the Hayes house.

Suddenly, he felt angry, bewildered, and very vulnerable. The refuge and tranquility he had established with his uncomplicated lifestyle was being disrupted. Personal schedules and activities were being checked. Relationships were in question. Pasts were being exposed and analyzed. Private lives were being turned upside down, and Matt found himself right in the middle of it all. And he was angry at himself, angry for not saying no when Ben asked him to help with the interviews the next morning.

"Why, couldn't I just say I don't want to get involved in this?" But Matt knew the answer. That damned dream. Did he really feel responsible because he dreamed this calamity?

When Matt approached his house, he felt reassured by the warm glow reflected on the snow. A light sensor had switched on the outside lights. His gloved hand awkwardly unzipped the pocket of his ski suit and retrieved a key. As he pushed the front door open, he recognized the sound of two familiar thumps as that of Spencer and Aslan descending from some favorite perch. Soon two furry, warm bodies wrapped themselves around Matt's legs in appreciation of his return.

"Hey, guys. Bet you're hungry. Let's see how you like chicken and artichokes. It's Pete's favorite dish...or so Ignatius says."

Matt watched with amusement as the cats slowly, delicately ate the chicken. However, the finicky felines carefully avoided the particles of artichokes that Ignatius had inadvertently included. When Matt had secured the house, he walked into his room to discover two large balls of fur, one black and one orange, curled up tightly on his bed.

"Thank heavens for the king-size," he said as he raised his arms and struggled out of his thermal undershirt.

His sleep was erratic. Matt roused himself into wakefulness each time he feared that he was being pursued by macabre dreams that would enter his world through the dark tunnel of his subconscious. However, the satisfaction of one of Ignatius' delicious dinners and the exercise of the hike up the hill weakened Matt's reserve.

Matt began to drift. He'd always thought he would be afraid to float in the air with no anchor to the matter below. Yet he was levitating just above damp, rotting steps that were descending into a dark abyss. The steps spiraled downward and with every turn the smell grew stronger. Damp, rotting, like a swamp. He could hear a trickle of water. He was glad he was floating. A light appeared a short distance ahead. He must be reaching the bottom of the stairwell. The light illuminated an object in the distance. He floated closer. Now he could see it was a large, purple beach ball. But, wait! Suddenly, a cowboy belt materialized and wrapped itself around the beach ball. The belt tightened until the big ball assumed the shape of a figure eight. Life appeared to enter the figure eight. It writhed and coiled like a pile of wiggling squirming worms. Suddenly, two elephantine legs erupted from the bottom half of the eight, and a head exploded through the top of the figure. Matt was floating closer to the apparition. He had no control. Unruly reddish-gray hair suddenly sprouted from the newly grown head, and dirty combs with missing teeth attempted to contain the unruly locks. Clouds of cigarette smoke encircled the head. He floated closer. He could almost touch the ghastly thing.

"This can't be real. I don't know how to levitate, so I know it's a dream." Matt reached out. As he extended his hand, the newly formed head turned abruptly. Grand! He knew it was Grand. The wrinkled old face that was thrust toward Matt belonged to the abhorrent, abusive grandmother of little Autumn and Spring Reynolds.

Matt screamed. He tried to inject reason into his terrifying predicament. Surely that bloodcurdling outcry will awaken the cats, and they will bolt and screech, and that will wake me up.

But instead of the yowl of the cats, Matt heard a dreadful, ominous chortle exploding from the hideous mouth of the phantom Grand. Spittle dribbled down her chin. The cigarette appeared again between her dry, cracked lips. She inhaled deeply, audibly, then slowly lifted a grimy hand and removed the butt. A hideous smile crept across her wrinkled face.

"Here, honey, want a puff?" She thrust the cigarette toward Matt and began to laugh again, wildly, maniacally. "Here, honey." The burning tip of the cigarette moved closer and closer to Matt.

"No," shouted Matt. He could feel the heat of the fiery dot. It was almost on his cheek. "No! Not my face!"

"Here you go, honey!" Grand touched the burning butt to Matt's face and suddenly Matt exploded. Pieces of skin, bone, and clothing glided gently, silently, slowly down into the dank-smelling abyss.

Matt was grabbing, reaching. "I have to catch my arm...can't lose my foot....my hand. My clothes...catch the shoe...my arm. Help me! Help me! I can't breathe. My chest! Pressure...I can't breathe."

Something was pressing on Matt's chest. The weight felt tremendous. Terror made it impossible for Matt to move. He tried to open his eyes, but they didn't work. Damn! He warned himself to relax. This was only a dream. But what about the pressure on his chest? Was he having a heart attack? Concentrate on the eyes. Open the eyes. It was working.

Finally, yellow lights penetrated his eyelids. He found it difficult to focus. Why did he see small, round, yellow lights? Then, to his horror, Matt realized that the small yellow lights were eyes. Hadn't the dream ended? They were cat eyes. The eyes belonged to Spencer. The large, sleek, black cat was situated possessively on Matt's chest. His paws moved rhythmically up and down as he contentedly kneaded his resting place. He stared intuitively into Matt's eyes as if he too had viewed the nightmare and perceived unknown danger.

Tuesday Morning

    Matt waited as Ben made his way up the hill slowly and cautiously. He seemed to advance a little slower this morning. As he moved closer, Matt noticed deep lines around Ben's mouth and dark circles under his eyes. The unprecedented scowl on his face made Matt realize that the additional burden of a second death was beginning to affect Ben's usual sunny disposition. Matt was also exhausted by his nightmarish encounter with the grotesque and ghastly Grand.

    Matt was still angry with himself for having agreed to accompany Ben on these interviews. Again he wondered if he had come along because the dream made him feel responsible in some way. As he watched Ben's gradual ascent, he suddenly felt another concern. His motive for being here might be prompted by an undue feeling of responsibility, but what was Ben's motive for asking him to come along?

"Morning, Matthew," Ben raised a heavy hand in his direction. "I'm moving a little slower this morning."

"I know what you mean, Ben. It takes a lot of energy to get around in this snow. Wonder what the official accumulation is now?"

"Don't know. I've stopped listening to the weatherman. Never says anything I want to hear. Let me catch my breath."

The two men exhaled frosty clouds of moisture and silently surveyed the surroundings. Attractive little homes, complete with smoking chimneys and well-stocked pantries, were nestled gently in the snow. Everything appeared undisturbed, flawless, and free of any violation. Even yesterday's tracks had been covered by last night's snow. The untainted setting rendered no clue to the upheaval taking place in the lives of the people who lived in the little houses.

"Who do you want to talk with first?" Matt said.

"Let's try Jeffreys. Do you think the mother and father will be home? I don't see any tire tracks leading from their driveway."

"Well, they could have parked at the bottom of the hill...like you did."

"Makes sense, but I parked down here because I don't know the street. Afraid I'd end up in the ditch. Anyway, I hope the parents are there. I don't like questioning a young person without the parents being there."

They started in the direction of the white brick house. "By the way," said Matt, "why did you want me to come along this morning? You met my neighbors already. I don't see what else I can do."

"I know I've met them, Matthew. And I appreciate your helping me out the other day. But I realized after I met these people that I had some unforeseen problems."

"What's that?"

"I think the people I really need to talk to are real scared. I think they are pretty close to the breaking point."

"You must be talking about Sean Jeffreys and Mrs. Phillips."

"Right. That's another reason I hope the boy's parents are home. If the kid goes over the edge, I'd like someone there who might know how to help him. As for Mrs. Phillips...that one really troubles me. We didn't see enough of her to even guess at what to expect. You don't mind, do you? Coming along, I mean. I could use the moral support, too. It's my first murder case and all."

"Oh no, Ben. Glad to help out. I was just curious." Matt could have kicked his gutless ass.

When the door to the Jeffreys' house opened, the disheveled man who stood before them was in sharp contrast to the fastidiously dressed person who had greeted them on their last visit. Gone was his ostentatious appearance. John Jeffreys wore jeans. Wrinkles almost obliterated the crease that had been painstakingly pressed into the legs. The tail of the orange flannel shirt was spilling out of the beltless pants, and a thermal undershirt was visible at the neckline. His hair was unkempt, and his face unshaven. Glazed, bloodshot eyes peered at the two visitors.

"Morning, Ben...Matt. Saw you coming up the hill. Come on in. What can I do for you gentlemen on such a treacherous morning?"

Matt and Ben stepped into the warm room. Ben removed his hat and smiled. "Morning, Mr. Jeffreys."

"Please, call me John."

"Good morning, John. You're not working today?"

"No. I've been working overtime since the storm hit, and I just had to take some time off. We won't be much help if we burn out. What can I do for you?"

"Well, John," said Ben, "it's about the Autumn Hayes case. There have been some new developments, and I need to ask some more questions."

"Gosh, I really can't think of anything to add to what we've already told you. Remember, we said we didn't know them that well."

"Nevertheless, I'd appreciate a few minutes of your time."

Matt realized that John Jeffreys had not invited them to sit down. Matt recalled his unctuous demeanor at their last meeting. Now he stood nervously shuffling from one foot to the other.

"What kind of new developments, Mr. Day?" The voice was that of Elizabeth Jeffreys. She had crept into the room. The tall, shadowy figure stood motionlessly as she scrutinized the intruders. As usual, her face was expressionless. Her voice was monotone.

Matt and Ben greeted Elizabeth simultaneously. Then Ben said, "The new development is that Jim Hayes is dead." He paused to give emphasis to the statement and to search for any change of expression on Elizabeth Jeffreys' face. Her expression remained immutable. Her husband issued a gasp and steadied himself by grasping the edge of a table.

"Oh, God!" exclaimed John Jeffreys. "Won't this ever end?" He dropped into a nearby chair and covered his face with his hands.

"I'm so sorry, John," said Ben. "I didn't mean to be insensitive. I somehow got the impression from our last conversation that the Hayeses were just casual acquaintances."

Without speaking or modifying her expression, Elizabeth Jeffreys slinked a step closer.

John looked at his wife. "No. I'm sorry, Ben. Your first impression was correct. Jim and Autumn Hayes were only neighbors. It's just so disturbing to realize that people you know can die so quickly. It's just shocking. You'd think I'd get used to it working at a hospital. Well, you never get used to it. I just try to focus on the getting well part." He stopped abruptly, aware of his rambling.

They sat silently. Suddenly, six thousand screaming watts of hard rap music pounded the walls of an adjoining room. The men were jolted from their composure. Elizabeth did not flinch. Could nothing ruffle this woman? Matt thought.

"How did Jim Hayes die, Sheriff?" The volume of Elizabeth's voice increased, but the tone was unchanged. In competition with the local radio station's rap station, Ben shouted the information he had to date on Hayes' death. So intent was he on making himself heard that Ben did not notice when the music abruptly stopped, and he continued to shout his report.

The door to the adjacent room flew open and a boy threw himself into the room. "Stop it! Haven't you got any respect? Haven't you got any feelings? Stop talking about it. She's dead. Nothing can bring her back. Nothing! Please stop it."

The boy collapsed on the couch, grabbed his knees, and rocked back and forth, sobbing hysterically. "Okay, Mom,' thought Matt, "let's see you remain detached through that outburst."

"Sean, please," John babbled, "Ben, uh...Sean has not been well. This whole catastrophe has left him very disturbed. He is another reason Elizabeth and I decided not to go in today. Sean, please...Elizabeth, perhaps you could take Sean back to his room."

"No." Ben said unequivocally. "Excuse me, Mrs. Jeffreys, but I really need to talk to Sean." He stepped closer and kneeled on one leg. "Son, I can tell you are really upset by all this. Many people are upset. I'm getting phone calls all day long from Mrs. Hayes' friends. They just can't rest until they know what happened. Now I can understand their feelings, and that is why I'm here today. Please, can you tell me anything that would help me get some answers for her friends?"

"Sheriff, you can hardly expect a young boy to do your job for you. My husband or I can answer any questions you might put to Sean," Elizabeth's terse voice interjected.

"I don't want to talk to you or your husband." Ben said simply. "I already talked to you. I want to talk to Sean. And if I don't talk to him here, then I'll have to talk to him in my office." His voice remained soft and kind.

Finally, a reaction. A hard and determined look appeared on Elizabeth Jeffreys' face. Her rage was apparent. With fists clinched by her side, she rushed toward Ben and stood over him threateningly. "You leave him alone, Sheriff. He's just a child. I'm sick and tired of people thinking they can come in here and jerk Sean around just because he's young and inexperienced. If you intend to throw your weight around here you'll have to have the legal stuff to do it. You got a warrant? Have you? Well, then you don't have the right to question my son. No jerk-water Sheriff's going to come in my house and throw his weight around. See you in court..."

"Holy cow!" thought Ben. "This Mama is capable of coming to the most ferocious defense of her young."

Ben sat quietly and let Elizabeth run out of steam. When her outburst elicited no response from the Sheriff, she fell into embarrassed silence.

"Mrs. Jeffreys I don't blame you for being upset." Ben finally said. "You wouldn't be much of a mama if you didn't want to protect your son. If you would like to call your lawyer and have him come over, or meet us at the station, that's fine. I just wanted to make this as simple, as I could. Seems to me like Sean has been through a lot."

Elizabeth flopped onto the couch beside her son. "I'm sorry, Sheriff. I'm so damned tired and frustrated. I'm not thinking clearly." She paused, took a deep breath, and squared her shoulders. "Why don't we let Sean make this decision? He's getting old enough to make big decisions now." Matt detected a slit of a smile. "Sean, do you want to talk to the Sheriff about Mrs. Hayes?"

Sean stopped rocking. He dropped his knees and nodded his head. "I've got to talk about this, Mother. I can't take this shit anymore. I gotta talk about it." Matt's heart was breaking for the kid. He'd seen that helpless look on the twins' faces many times before.

"I met Autumn about a year ago," Sean began. "Her and her husband had this picnic-like at their house. They had just moved here and didn't know nobody or nothing so they gave this party. I didn't want to go 'cause there weren't no other kids going. But Mother said I had to," he shrugged, "Ended up that I was real glad I went. Autumn was something. She was the most beautiful girl I ever saw. I know she was older, but to me she was a girl. But that was only part of it. She was so kind and understood how I felt about things and all. At that party, I felt out of place. I didn't know how to talk about the stuff they were talking about and all. Anyway, Autumn, she sensed this right away. I'd gone back into the kitchen to get another soda, and she came in and put her hand on my arm and said, 'Sean, I'm sorry this is such a bore for you. I understand. Maybe just the two of us can get together sometime and get to know each other.' I remember that her hand felt so warm and soft. We got to seeing each other and all. Mostly when I came home from school. Her husband didn't care about her. He worked late every night, and my parents never got home till dark. Well, one thing led to another, and we had this real special relationship...I mean it was special...and loving...and I know what you're thinking. The age difference. But you're as young as you act, that's what Autumn always said. I know what you're thinking." Sean began to sputter.

"Sean, was this special relationship of a sexual nature?" Ben interrupted.

"Yes."

"You had a sexual relationship with Autumn Hayes?"

"Yes. And everything was going fine until last week. A guy never knows who is going to step right in and tear up his life. Sometimes it's the person you least expect."

The tears gushed down his ashen cheeks again. Ben waited patiently. "It was his fault. All his fault." Sean pointed an accusing finger at John Jeffreys. "The day the snow was predicted, they let school out early so the busses could make their route before the storm really hit. I was so happy. That meant that I would have extra time with Autumn. When I walked by my house I didn't see a car. I went straight to Autumn's house. She never locked the door in the afternoon, so I went on in. I heard voices and thought it was her husband. I was turning to go back outside when who should come bouncing down the steps but him." Sean pointed to John Jeffreys again. "And to make matters worse, Autumn was right behind him, naked. Man, I lost it. I mean, I really lost it. I called them everything I could think of. I threw things and screamed and cussed. That damned dog started yapping, and I kicked the shit out of him. Then *he* tried to give me these stupid excuses...I don't even remember what they were. But they were stupid. Tried to calm me down. But do you know what hurt me the most? Do you want to know? He's my father! My father, for crap sake!

"When I came home, I had to wait for Mother to get home. Then I went through the whole thing with her. He just sat there...didn't say nothing. Then I had to listen to them battle it out. They didn't even care about me. That son of a bitch. The only one who ever cared about me was Autumn.

"So that's my story. The next thing I knew, you were over here telling us that Autumn is murdered. It's a nightmare! A nightmare I'll never wake up from."

Sean dropped his head into his hands. Matt cringed at the perversity to which the boy had been subjected. Matt wanted to go to him and hold him the way he had held Chad and Garth when their mother died. He wanted to tell him that time would make it better. But Matt sat still. He waited for Ben to make the first move.

Ben reached over and took the hands of the pitiful young man much as one would those of a child. "Son," he said almost inaudibly, "did you kill Autumn Hayes?"

Sean lifted his head and gazed straight into Ben's eyes. "No sir. I did not kill Autumn Hayes."

Ben patted the boy's knee. "I'm so sorry you've had to go through all this Sean. Real sorry. That's enough for now. If you think of anything else that might help in the investigation, please let me know. I might be asking you more questions as the investigation progresses. John, I'll be needing to get a statement from you, and from you, too, Mrs. Jeffreys. But right now we're going to leave and let this family have a little peace." He stood up. "Thank you, John. Thank you, Mrs. Jeffreys."

"Call me Elizabeth." she said.

"Thank you, Elizabeth."

Matt felt a tremendous sense of relief as he and Ben stepped out into the clean, crisp air. The intensity of the interview combined with his dream about the repulsive

Grand had left him zapped of all energy. He wasn't sure he could handle another session this morning.

"Well, Ben, what do you think?"

"What I think, Matthew, is that I needn't have worried about a suspect to replace Jim Hayes. Right in there," he jerked a thumb in the direction of the white-brick house, "I've got three good suspects. But I don't mind telling you, I sure hope it ain't that boy. I still have a lot of questions to ask him."

CHAPTER 17

In spite of overwhelming fatigue, Ben found that the information obtained from Sean Jeffreys provided him with the incentive to continue his investigation immediately. Undeterred, he and Matt plunged through the snow in the direction of the Phillips' house.

"Matt, you know I talked with your friends in Virginia."

Matt was taken aback. "Caryn too?"

"Yes, Ms. Shipley *and* Mr. Axelrod. Seem to be real nice folks, Matt."

"Watch the use of that word *nice*. Remember how sardonic Ignatius becomes when you speak of someone being *nice*."

"Yeah...well, regardless of what 'Natius would say, she's a real nice lady."

"What did Caryn have to say...and Brian, too?"

Ben smiled. "I mostly had two questions to ask them. Caryn gave me the name and phone number of Jim Hayes' father. He lives in Texas, just outside of Austin. I called him this morning and broke the bad news. He was real torn up, of course, but assured me he would take care of all the arrangements as soon as the body is released when the weather breaks. He volunteered to do the same for Autumn if we couldn't find any of her relatives.

"Neither Caryn or Brian knew where I could find Spring. Brian said she was just gone one day...left

Randolph County, North Carolina, right after Autumn did. And the mother...well, nobody ever saw her again after the night she dumped the girls at Grand's. So I struck out there. Guess I'll just let Mr. Hayes take care of both of them. It's up to the Doc to say when."

The men arrived at the Philips' house. As they stepped up on the porch, the door sprung open. A smiling, amiable Mr. Phillips filled the doorway. The look of hopelessness and depression apparent at their last visit had disappeared. He was clean shaven, and although his clothes had not been pressed, they were clean. This man resembled more closely the neighbor who had been so supportive and accommodating to Matt during his mother's long illness.

"Come on in, fellows! I seen you going in the Jeffreys', and I thought you might be coming to see me next. Glad to see you. I'm starting to get cabin fever...haven't worked in several days. Center's open, but not many people are showing up." He was walking down the hallway, leading them toward the kitchen. "I made a fresh pot of coffee and stuck some Pepperidge Farm coffee cake in the oven. Using a lot of store-bought stuff now since I'm the chief cook."

Gospel music filled the house, as it had on their last visit, but this time the volume was fixed at a more tolerable level. Matt noticed that Ida Phillips was at her station in the living room. This time, instead of rocking, she paced back and forth in cadence to the popular quartet's recording, "Whispering Hope, Oh, how welcome thy voice..."

Jesse was in a gregarious mood, and appeared to be oblivious to the sound of the hymn that was repeated over and over. He talked about his favorite brands of frozen foods, the difficulty of keeping a supply of dry wood, the saga of his frozen water pipes, the latest news on the blizzard. It seemed that he was eager to discuss anything that came to mind, except his wife's aberration.

He served Matt and Ben large, steaming hot mugs of strong coffee and generous portions of cake. Pulling a third chair up to the table, he said, "Fill me in, Sheriff. How is your investigation going?"

Ben slowly sipped his coffee. Then, lowering his cup, he plunged headlong into the account of the discovery of Jim Hayes' body and the notification of his father. He inquired again if Mr. Phillips had remembered anything that might help them locate Autumn Hayes' family. Jesse Phillips had no such recollection.

Then Ben cautiously broached the question of interviewing Mrs. Phillips. "Mr. Phillips, I hope you can understand now that it is real important for me to get as much information about the Hayes couple as I can. So I'd like to question your wife this morning."

"Sheriff, I can't see how she can be of any help to you. She doesn't make any sense. All it would do is just upset her, and..."

"Mr. Phillips, I understand that she might be easily upset, that is why I am willing to talk to her here instead of down at the office. But if you'd rather bring her into town...maybe have your lawyer there...that would be up to you. I'll let you make that choice."

Jesse Phillips arose and walked slowly toward the hall. His stance revealed his feeling of frustration. "No, Sheriff, you can talk to her here. But please be kind to her. She's like a little child. Anything can set her off. Then other times, she won't say a word." He led Matt and Ben in the direction of the music.

When the men entered the living room, Ida Phillips was still pacing pitifully up and down the room as the gospel group sang of hope. Jesse Phillip cleared his throat. "Ida, you remember Matt Murray, and this is Benjamin Day. Ben is the Sheriff, and he is here to ask you some questions," he shouted.

Ida Phillips showed no sign that she was mindful of anyone having entered the room. She twisted a shredded tissue as she marched back and forth, simply stepping around the men who stood in her path.

Matt spoke of familiar topics in an effort to interrupt her ritualistic behavior. "Mrs. Phillips, remember me? I'm Matthew Murray, your neighbor. You used to visit me regularly when my mother was alive. You and she used to go shopping together, and you talked on the telephone for hours. Remember how long you used to talk on the phone? I also remember all the delicious meals you brought us when she got sick. You make the best lemon pie. I don't know what I would have done without your help..." Matt realized that his dialogue was not breaking through her confusion.

Ben motioned for Jesse to lower the volume of the music. Then the Sheriff stepped into her path.

"Miz Phillips, I'm Benjamin Day. I'm the Sheriff who's investigating the death of your neighbor, Autumn Hayes. I wonder if I could ask you a few questions."

Ida Phillips abruptly halted her march. Her face was less than a foot from Ben's. Her vacant gaze was reflected in his eyes. Then, after a brief hesitation, she simply stepped around him and continued marching. Ben looked at Matt hopelessly. Matt shook his head. Then suddenly from behind the Sheriff came a deafening, shriek as Ida Phillips substituted her voice for that of the gospel quartet. Matt and Ben jumped as the diabolical sound pervaded the entire house. Jesse Phillips rushed toward his wife. He wrapped his arm around her shoulder protectively and whispered to her inaudibly. Matt and Ben slowly left the room and returned to the kitchen. Both men were shaken and waited wordlessly for Jesse to join them.

"I'm sorry, fellas," said Jesse as he entered the room. "I was afraid that would happen. Can't ever tell what might set her off."

Matt spoke, "Mr. Phillips, when did she get this sick? Can you tell us what happened?"

"I'll pour you another cup of coffee."

"No thanks," said Ben. "Like Matt said, can you tell us what happened to your wife?"

Jesse looked helpless. "I guess it all started a long time ago. You see, Ida has two sisters. All three sisters are married. For some unknown reason, it had been impossible for any of them to get pregnant. Finally, Viola, the middle sister, got pregnant and had this little girl. The other two sisters remained childless. You with me on this so far?"

Both Matt and Ben nodded. "The new mother and the two doting aunts adored that little girl," Jesse went on. "They worshiped the ground she walked on. Anything she wanted, she got. You'd think that she'd grow up to be spoiled and selfish, but, no. She was the sweetest little ol' gal you'd ever want to meet. They sent her through college, and while she was there, she met a young man. It was a beautiful wedding, and the bride looked like a baby doll. The three sisters just bawled and carried on. But when the wedding was over, they was just as happy as doodle bugs for that little ol' gal. Still kept an eye on her and helped her whenever she needed it. There was one thing they couldn't help her with, however. Seemed like the girl done inherited the curse of the sisters. She couldn't have a child. This just broke her heart and the hearts of her mother and two aunts. I can remember Ida gave her a little old dog for Christmas one year, and she just hugged it and cried and named it Baby. My wife and her two sisters cried right along with her. The one thing that little ol' gal wanted most, and they couldn't give it to her. About a year ago she died. It was liked she gave up on life. Just couldn't stand the pain no more, I guess. The three sisters near 'bout went crazy, and Ida ain't been right since. The doctor says it's depression brought on by the trauma of her niece's death. I don't know. I just try to accept what they say and do the best I can. Ida is on medication. And some days are worse than others. Today is a bad day. Been bad ever since the death across the way there. Guess it brought back too many memories."

    Matt expelled a breath he appeared to have been holding throughout the story of Ida Phillips' illness. "Mr. Phillips, I'm so sorry. What can I do? I'd like to do something to help you like you helped me with Mom."

    "Thanks, Matt. I can't think of anything right now. Maybe when she goes to see the doctor in Nashville, you might drive us sometime."

    "Sure, be glad to."

    Ben returned the conversation to the investigation. "Mr. Phillips, I too, would like to express my regrets that your wife is so ill. Perhaps you'd try again to help me out. Now, did she act any different that day of the murder? Did she say anything...regardless of how insignificant or irrelevant it may seem to you...did she say anything that would lead you to believe she may have seen or heard something unusual?"

"No, Ben, she sure has not. I've thought about that a lot. I can't think of anything that would indicate she saw or heard anything."

"Well, since you said she had bad days and better days, would you be alert on the better days? If she says anything you feel would be helpful...anything at all...call me right away. Thank you again, and I hope we didn't upset Miz Phillips too much."

"Okay, Ben. I'll keep in touch. Good to see you, Matt. Please come over. I get awful lonesome here."

"You bet, Mr. Phillips. Believe me I know what you're going through. I'll see you soon. Call if you need anything."

Matt and Ben were outside once more inhaling the cold fresh air. They quietly made their way to the road, allowing their ears to adjust to the welcomed silence.

"I suppose I'll wait till morning to talk to the Jeffreys family again. Don't think anybody's going very far in this weather. Besides, I got Dexter keeping the neighborhood under pretty close surveillance."

"Really? I didn't know that."

"Yeah, can't take no chances. Say, you wouldn't want to go with me to see the Jeffreys family tomorrow morning, would you?"

"Are you kidding? I certainly do. After this morning, now I'm real anxious to see how this thing plays out."

"Me too, Matthew. We got something here, and I'm not sure what. I can't connect the dots yet. Thanks for coming along. Two heads are better than one and all that stuff..."

"Same time, same place?"

"Yeah, same time, same place."

Matt was experiencing an incredible emotional overload. As he sank into the leather chair, he marveled that his feelings of apprehension were now replaced by an inexplicable curiosity. He lifted the telephone and punched Ignatius' number. As he counted the rings, he was joined by the two lithe felines. Spencer settled gently into Matt's lap, and Aslan assumed a regal pose on the foot of the recliner, yellow eyes staring expectantly at the instrument in Matt's hand. Ring, ring.

"Yeah?"

"Hey Nate...Matt. Thought I'd call and fill you in on what's happening."

"Great. What's happening?"

Matt admitted to the curiosity that now engrossed him as he recounted the morning's events.

"So Nate, what does your objective eye make of all this?"

"She was one contentious bitch wasn't she? I recall an old saying. It goes, 'If a woman don't get the man she wants--God help the man she gets.' Well, God help Jim and Sean and John and any other poor bastard who was sucked in by that woman. As for poor Ida Phillips, I feel real sorry for both her and her husband. Too bad all this had to happen right in front of her home. So what happens next?"

"Ben will talk to John and Elizabeth Jeffreys again tomorrow morning. I'm going with him."

"You're okay with that?"

"Yeah."

"Fine. I'm glad to see that you're dealing with this. Some things just can't be explained, Matt. I'm talking about the dreams, you know."

"I've really been working on not feeling responsible for any of this because of the dream. Discussing things with you has really helped."

Igatius steered the conversation away from the dream. "Why don't you and Ben come by for lunch? Black bean soup and buttermilk pie."

"I don't know about Ben, but sounds good to me. Is this another one of Pete's favorite dishes?"

"Say, Matt, did Ben say anything else about Pete? You know, about who will get him."

"Sure didn't, Nate."

"Well, I'm not giving him up without one hell of a fight. See you tomorrow."

"Yeah, see ya."

CHAPTER 18

Matt and Ben stood on the Jeffreys' front porch. They huddled against the wind and waited for John Jeffreys' response to their knock. Matt was in the midst of extending Ignatius' lunch invitation to Ben when the door flew open assisted by a gust of frigid wind mixed with snow. John Jeffreys fumblingly caught the door before it could slam against the wall.

"Matt...Ben. Come on in. Won't this snow ever quit? This is the biggest snowstorm I remember since I was a child. Seems as we had bigger snowstorms back when I was a child..." John was helping his visitors remove their coats, and appeared to be unaware of his rambling.

John looked far less harried than when Matt and Ben had last seen him. He was clean shaved and wore neatly pressed jeans and a flannel shirt unbuttoned enough to expose a hairy chest. A gold neck chain flashed against his unseasonable tan and a matching gold watch peeped from under the long sleeves each time he raised his arms. As if oblivious to the cold, he chose to wear no socks with his tan, leather boat shoes.

He invited the men into the living room and motioned them to large matching stuffed chairs. John joined them before the blazing fire.

He prattled on. "We did have quite a bit of snow when I was a kid, though. I can remember one time we had a big winter storm, and my parents bought me new boots. When I stepped outside, my feet sank, and the snow was so deep that it came up above the top of my boots and filled them with snow. Scared me to death. I thought..."

"John, I'm sure that Mr. Murray and Mr. Day did not come here this morning to hear stories of your childhood adventures. Good morning, gentlemen." With face thrust forward, Elizabeth Jeffreys came into the room from the kitchen. Her demeanor revealed that she was reestablishing the formal atmosphere that had existed before Ben had questioned Sean. She continued, "May I get you something to drink before we begin? I have a fresh pot of coffee, and I just baked some bran muffins."

"Good morning, Miz Jeffreys. Yes, some coffee would be nice, but I'll pass on the muffins," said Ben.

"Coffee sounds good," agreed Matt. "I'll skip the muffins, too."

"Well, all right," said Elizabeth as if disappointed. She disappeared into the kitchen and returned with steaming mugs of coffee. She joined the group assembled in front of the fireplace.

Ben spoke, "How's the boy?"

"He is sleeping," Elizabeth answered. "We gave him a light sedative, and he should sleep another three or four hours. I hope our interview will be over by then. Sheriff, since you ask about Sean, there is something that I would like to discuss with you. I would like as much assurance as you can possibly give me that the knowledge you have and will acquire in this investigation pertaining to this family will not become food for the gossip mongers of this town. Sean has been through a lot. Lord only knows how all of this is going to affect him anyway." John cast his eyes toward the floor. "Realistically, I know you have a job to do, but so do I. I am Sean's mother, and I feel a need to protect him as much as possible. Children can be cruel, Mr. Day, especially teenagers. If the kids at the high school ever find out about Sean and that woman, the ridicule will be unbearable for him."

"Miz Jeffreys, I understand how you feel. All I can say is that it is not my intention to collect information for any purpose other than that of solving the murder of Autumn Hayes. Any coincidental information I come across in the process will be treated with the utmost confidentiality. Only if it has a direct bearing on the case will it be used."

"Thank you, Sheriff."

"On the other hand, Miz Jeffreys, if it does have a bearing on the murder, in other words, if someone here is involved, then that information will become part of the record. Until I make that determination, I am okay with talking with you folks here at your home off the record. Let me remind you, however, if at any time you become uncomfortable with this, let me know and you can call your lawyer. Understood?"

"Certainly, Sheriff. For the time being, I would like for you to continue your questioning here." Matt noticed that since Elizabeth had re-entered the scene, John had contributed nothing to the conversation. Apparently, Ben had surmised the same thing.

"Now, having taken care of that," said Ben, "I would like to talk to both you and your husband alone. Could we start with Mr. Jeffreys?"

"Now that I have your assurance of confidentiality, Sheriff, I have no objections at all to private conferences."

She arose and shuffled toward the kitchen. "I'll be in the laundry room, ironing. There's more coffee...and the bran muffins, of course."

As Elizabeth left the room, life seemed to reenter the body of John Jeffreys. He raised his head and expelled a deep breath. "She really loves Sean, you know."

"She should," said Ben. "He seems like a great kid."

"I love him, too, Sheriff. Do you think that I would have ever let this happen if I had known that Sean was going over there? I could never hurt him that way."

"Mr. Jeffreys, it's not my job to pass judgment on you as a parent. I'm here to learn anything I can that will help me find the murderer of Autumn Hayes. Shall we get started?"

"Sure. What would you like to know?" He slipped to the edge of his chair, dark eyes peering directly into Ben's.

Ben sighed. He extracted a pad and pen from his pocket, leaned back into the plush stuffed chair and said, "Why don't you just start off by telling me how you first met Autumn Hayes?"

"What I told you yesterday about that is the truth, Sheriff. The Hayeses moved here last spring, and on the Fourth of July they invited the neighbors over to their house for an open house. They had a barbecue, and that was the first time I met either of them...Jim or Autumn."

"Do you recall when you next saw Autumn Hayes?"

"Yes. It was about a couple of weeks later--I'm not sure exactly when. I know it wasn't the next week 'cause we took a family trip to Indiana. That's where my wife is from. Her mother lives there and is in bad health, so we try to get…"

"Could we get back to Autumn Hayes?" interrupted Ben. "Now the question was, when did you see Autumn Hayes for the second time, and you think then that it was approximately two weeks later. Is that right?"

"Yes, approximately two weeks."

"What were the circumstances of this meeting, John?"

"Ah...well, the circumstances of the meeting were that we were going to become lovers."

"Excuse me, John. I must have missed something here. You met Autumn Hayes on the Fourth of July?"

"Yes."

"Two weeks later, without having any other meetings, you meet her in order to become lovers? Is this right?"

"Well, yes, it is. But that was only after the phone call."

"You called Miz Hayes?"

"No, she called me."

"Okay, let's try it again. You meet on the Fourth of July, she calls you, and you meet to become lovers. Do I understand this right?"

"Yes, I know it sounds strange. It always does when I try to give precise answers to questions. I have a problem knowing what to include and what to leave out."

"I tell you what, John. Why don't I just sit here and let you tell me in your own words about how you got mixed up with Autumn Hayes." Ben leaned back, crossed an ankle over his knee, took a deep breath, and prepared to be there for a while.

"We were invited to this barbecue that the Hayeses had on the Fourth of July last year. I'd never met Autumn before then. In spite of everything that has happened, I still think that she was one of the most captivating women I've ever seen. First of all, she was beautiful. She was tall and tan, and her fingernails and toenails were painted the same deep vibrant red. She didn't wear any lipstick...she didn't need to emphasize those full, voluptuous lips." Matt cleared his throat. John glared at the interruption.

"Sorry," said Matt, his voice cracking.

John continued, "I remember that she wore this outfit that reflected an Indian motif... a Native American motif, that is." Ben and Matt smiled at John's attempt to be politically correct even under the circumstances. "The skirt was long and made of some kind of thin, gauze-like kind of material. You could see right through it. And she didn't wear a slip. The design of the skirt was in brown, gold, and green. The gold blouse was one of those off-the-shoulder deals that was cut way down in front, showing more cleavage than you'd expect to see at a backyard barbecue...or so my wife said when we got home." His finger traced the front of his shirt as he indicated the low cut of the blouse.

He continued. "But it wasn't just her provocative appearance that caught my attention. She had this way about her. She made me think that everything I said was important. When I talked with her, she looked at me as if she were hanging on my every word. Like...I'm not a good joke-teller, but she would laugh at my corny attempts until tears came in her eyes. Then she'd get everyone's attention and say, 'Everyone, everyone...you've just got to hear this'.' And even if I screwed up the joke, Autumn laughed so hard that it was contagious. Soon the whole crowd roared. Several times that night she went out of her way to make me feel acknowledged and included. I was flattered by the attentions of this beautiful, sumptuous woman. Several times during the day, she patted my hand or gently brushed against me. Once as we were standing at the table, her knee touched my leg...but I thought that all of this was accidental. I never thought of it as intentional. I just enjoyed the day and the attentions of a beautiful, desirable woman."

"Was Miz Jeffreys aware of this attention?"

"If she were, she didn't say anything about it. The only comment she made was about the cleavage, you know, when we got home."

"Now you say you had your first rendezvous with Autumn Hayes after a phone call she made to you?"

"Right."

"Exactly what did she say?"

"Well, I can't remember her exact words. When I realized who was calling me, my heart beat so loud that I could hardly hear what she was saying. I remember she sounded so friendly and matter-of-fact, just like she called me every day. She made small talk. I was too dumbfounded to think of anything to say. Then she said that Jim, her husband, was out of town, and she couldn't get one of her windows to close. She wanted me to come over and fix it."

"So?" Ben prompted.

"So I went, and that was our first time alone together."

"Just a few questions here, John. Where were you when Autumn called you that first time?"

"At work at the hospital."

"Could Miz Jeffreys have overheard that conversation?"

"No. I was in my private office."

"Could anyone else have overheard it?"

"No. I answered the phone myself and no one else was in the office."

"No one could have listened in?"

"No. My office is encased with a glass front wall. I could see that no one was in the outer office."

"Weren't you afraid that your wife might go home and see your car in the neighbor's yard?"

"No. I parked in the Hayes' garage that day and from then on. Autumn told me to."

"Then, you are quite confident that your wife was unaware of your relationship with Autumn Hayes until Sean told her?"

"Yes."

"How often did you visit Autumn Hayes?"

"About once a week, usually at my lunch time."

"And you had no idea that Sean was also keeping company with your neighbor, Autumn Hayes."

"No, I didn't, Ben. I swear." John Jeffreys' face took on a somber expression. "If I had had even the faintest notion that she was messing around with Sean, do you think I would have continued to go over there? That's obscene!

What kind of father would I be to share her bed with my own son?"

"Then you're telling me that the first knowledge you had of a relationship between Sean and Autumn was the day he walked in and found you with Autumn...the day before the murder."

"Right. I'll never forget that day. I remember starting down those steps. We were laughing, Autumn and me. Suddenly the door burst open and Sean charged into the room. I remember that his mouth was open, as if he were going to call out. He had this smile all across his face. Then it was as if someone took his face and turned it upside down. He looked at me, then at Autumn. She didn't have any clothes on. Then he just went berserk. I remember that the whole house reverberated with screams, moans, cries, swearing. I tried to restrain him. He was as strong as two men. We fought. At one point his resistance subsided for just a moment. I looked up at Autumn, who was still standing on the steps, still naked, making no attempt to cover herself. It seemed that she was posed there totally unashamedly. And then I saw something I'll never forget."

"What did you see, John?" Both Matt and Ben leaned forward.

John continued. "She started to smile. First it was a little grin. Then her mouth turned up and the grin evolved into a mocking, contemptible smile." He paused. "I just froze. Finally, Sean broke loose and ran home. I got in my car and came on home. He wouldn't let me in, so I removed the hinges from the door between the garage and kitchen and lifted the door off. That's how I got into the house. He wouldn't open his bedroom door, so I just waited until

Elizabeth came home. That was the longest two hours of my life. I didn't know what was going on inside of Sean's room. All I could hear was that crazy music of his. It was so loud that it jolted the whole house. When Elizabeth came home, Sean burst from his room and blurted out the whole disgusting mess. Then, I suppose, the rest is history. Elizabeth and I went at it for hours. I guess Sean was right. We forgot about him and his pain. Will he ever forgive me? Will I ever forgive myself?" John Jeffreys dropped his face into his hands and began to shake his head.

Ben waited for John to regain control of himself. John finally lifted his head and stared at the men through bloodshot eyes. "John," Ben said softly as if to a frightened child, "to your knowledge, did Sean leave this house between the time this scene with your wife occurred and the time when Autumn Hayes' body was found?"

"Oh no, Ben, he didn't. He couldn't have left here without either Elizabeth or I seeing him. We stayed up practically the entire night *discussing* this mess."

"Could he have gone out of the window?"

"No. There's a storm window that must be removed from the outside."

"Now about Miz Jeffreys. Did she leave the house between the time you were arguing and the time Autumn Hayes' body was found?"

"What? No! She most certainly did not. Now listen, Ben, my family had nothing to do with the death of Autumn Hayes. Guilty of poor judgment. Guilty of not being considerate of each other. Guilty of...I don't know what else. But not guilty of murder. Neither Elizabeth nor Sean left this house that night."

"And what about you, John? Did you leave this house that night?"

"NO!"

"Did you kill Autumn Hayes?"

"Oh, God no!" John Jeffreys had once again dropped his face into his hands and was sobbing. "I couldn't do that. I couldn't kill her, Ben." Then in a whisper he added, "I loved her. Heaven help me. I loved her."

Matt turned away from the weeping man and glanced toward the opposite end of the room. The slumped figure of Elizabeth Jeffreys filled the doorway to the kitchen. Matt recalled the hard, determined look that had appeared on Elizabeth's face as she rose to her son's defense. He saw no sign that this kind of protective reaction was likely to occur on behalf of her husband. She lifted her hand and covered her mouth as if suppressing any sound. When she stepped back and disappeared into the kitchen, she was gone so quickly, so stealthily, that she might have been an apparition.

CHAPTER 19

John Jeffreys left the living room to summons Elizabeth to her conference. Matt took advantage of his absence to inform Ben that Elizabeth had been standing in the kitchen doorway at the end of John's interview and had probably overheard John's declaration of love for Autumn.

"You know, I feel sorta sorry for the *iron lady*," Matt said. "She's taken a lot of hits lately. In spite of that austere exterior, she's out there dealing with her son's sexuality and her husband's infidelity with the same sort of dread and anxiety that any mother and wife would feel. Yet, she still irons her husband's Levis, attends to and comforts her distressed son, and bakes bran muffins for the Sheriff who is coming in to question the whole family in a murder investigation. I gotta say, Elizabeth can handle a lot. But when John said he loved Autumn, I never saw such torment on her face. I hope that John doesn't overestimate what his wife is able to contend with."

"I hope he doesn't overestimate what she's *willing* to contend with," Ben added.

As they spoke, Elizabeth skulked back into the living room and joined them by the fire. She folded herself into the chair that John had just vacated. Placing her hands in her lap and thrusting her face forward, she said in a commanding voice, "Now, how can *I* help you, Sheriff?"

"I'd like to ask you a few questions about the Fourth of July barbecue which was given at the Hayes' house last year," said Ben. "Was your entire family invited to the cook-out?"

"Yes."

"How was the invitation extended?"

"By phone."

"Who took the phone call?"

"I did."

"Who actually made the call? Was it Autumn or Mr. Hayes?"

"Autumn Hayes."

"Was that the first time you'd ever had a conversation with Autumn Hayes?"

"Yes."

Ben realized that, unlike John Jeffreys, Elizabeth Jeffreys was not inclined to embellish nor elaborate. "Mrs. Jeffreys, you told me the other day that you were not a friend of Autumn Hayes because you had nothing in common with her. Could you explain a little more fully what you meant by that?"

"Yes. Since Autumn Hayes was the hostess, I tried several times to engage her in conversation on such topics as the headaches of building a new house and landscaping a yard. I inquired how she liked living in Winchester. I asked her about her previous job, having in mind the idea that we might be able to use her at the hospital. But it soon became apparent that Autumn had interests other than that kind of small talk."

"What other kinds of interest do you mean?"

"As far as conversation was concerned, she appeared to prefer topics which would capture the attention of the entire party as opposed to a one-on-one type conversation with me. She seemed particularly determined to hold the interest of the men." She looked squarely at Matt. "As I recall, Matt, you too were privileged to be a recipient of her attention earlier in the day. I also noticed that you were not very receptive to her *wiles*."

Ben glanced at Matt, who cleared his throat. "I suppose I was...for a while. However, I just interpreted her behavior as that of an over-zealous hostess, concerned that no one be excluded."

Elizabeth snorted.

"Let's get back to you now, Mrs. Jeffreys," Ben said. "Were you aware that she was showing unusual attention to your husband, John?"

Elizabeth's eyes diverted his gaze. "Yes," she almost whispered. "I was very much aware that she was showing John unusual attention. I'm not really sure I can explain this, Sheriff, but John has changed a lot in the twenty years that we have been married. When I met him, he was like a boy. He looked like a teenager. He was short and thin. He possessed few of the social graces, and he certainly didn't know how to dress. When we became engaged, I began to help him address these weaknesses. Consequently, he developed more poise and self confidence. When he was offered the job at the hospital, we were both ecstatic. The rest speaks for itself. I watched him grow, Sheriff. He became confident, self assured, successful. I suppose that I viewed Autumn's flirtation with my husband as harmless...just another experience that would bolster his self-esteem even more. I most certainly did not think it would come to this."

"Did you have any idea that your husband was seeing Autumn Hayes?"

"You mean did I have any idea that John was having an affair with Autumn Hayes?"

"Yes."

"The answer is no, Sheriff. I never gave Autumn Hayes another thought from that day until the day that Sean told me that he had walked in on their little escapade."

"Now, Mrs. Jeffreys," Ben looked at her, "did you have any knowledge that Sean was..."

"Having a relationship with Autumn Hayes?" She leaned forward, and the look in her eyes equaled the intensity of his. "Do you think for one minute if I had known that Sean was having sex with that woman that I would not have put a stop to it once and for all?"

"Yes, Mrs. Jeffreys. I do think you would have put a stop to it once and for all, which leads me to my next question. Did you leave this house between the time you and John had that showdown about Autumn and the next morning when her body was found?"

Elizabeth's eyes never left his face. "No," she said in a hoarse voice.

"Did John leave this house between the time of your argument and the time that Autumn's body was found?"

"No."

"Did your son, Sean, leave the house between the time of your argument with your husband and the time that Autumn's body was found?"

"Definitely, *NO!*"

"Did you hear or see anything that evening or the following morning that could help in the investigation of this case?"

"Quite frankly, Sheriff, I've been too busy trying to keep my family from falling apart. I've given as little consideration to Autumn Hayes as I can."

"I may take that as a no, then?"

"You may take that as an unequivocal no. I shall not contend that my husband is not to blame in the matter of the affair. That is something that he and I shall have to deal with. But believe me when I say that there is not a violent bone in his body. It is unfathomable that he could have murdered anyone."

"Mrs. Jeffreys, law enforcement officers will tell you that most everyone is capable of violence, given the right circumstances."

"Well, that might make an interesting fireside debate some evening, but right now I am preoccupied with attending to my family. And I know our limits."

Elizabeth arose in an effort to end the interview. "Now, Sheriff, if there are no more questions, you'll have to excuse me. I must check on Sean."

Ben didn't move. "There is one thing more, Mrs. Jeffreys. If he is up to it, I would like to speak to Sean, too." Elizabeth's face turned dark. She opened her mouth to protest. "Just briefly, Mrs. Jeffreys. Very briefly. I just need to ask him a couple of questions."

Yielding to the inevitable, Elizabeth said, "All right, Sheriff...if he is awake. We may as well get this over with. But briefly, you understand. I'll intervene if I feel this is too upsetting for him."

As Sean Jeffreys entered the room, the men noticed that his face was pale and gaunt. He appeared to be much thinner than they remembered. His eyes were glazed and red. His expression was empty and his coordination was poor. Elizabeth walked beside him protectively.

"Sheriff, I'm not sure Sean should do this. He had a sedative, and he is still very groggy."

"No," Sean's speech was slurred. "I want to get this over with. Let's do it now."

"Sean, I'll be glad to come back," volunteered Ben.

"No," Sean repeated. "I'm all right. I'd rather talk now."

"Mrs. Jeffreys, I know you want to be here, but there might be some things that Sean may feel embarrassed to discuss if his mother is present. I'm sure you know what I mean. I'll leave it up to the two of you, and I promise that this will be brief."

Elizabeth started to protest. "I don't want to talk about this in front of you, Mom," Sean said. "It's bad enough to have to talk to anyone, but I don't want you to hear."

"Sean, I'm concerned about--"

"Please, Mom. I can't talk about this with you here. Not yet, anyway."

Elizabeth turned reluctantly. "Very well, Sean. I'll be in the kitchen." She shot a sinister look at Ben that warned him she would be keeping a nearby vigil.

Ben slipped to the edge of his chair. "Son, how do you feel?"

"Empty...just plain empty. I wish I could wake up and find that this is a terrible nightmare."

"The offer still stands to do this another time."
"No. Now."
"Okay. I'll be as brief as possible. When was the first time you met Autumn Hayes?"
"I told you already. It was at the stupid Fourth of July barbecue that the Hayeses had--when they first moved here. I didn't want to go. Mom insisted. She likes for me to do that sort of thing for the *social experience*. I'd much rather have been with my friends out at Tims Ford Park."
"What was it like when you got there?"
"Boring. I'd rather have been anywhere but there." Sean's voice was angry, resentful.
"And you met Autumn Hayes then?" Ben asked returning to the objective of his questioning.
"Yes." His eyes filled with tears.
"Can you tell me about it?"
"Yes. I couldn't think of anything to talk to those people about. I never felt so awkward in all my life. There wasn't one single person my age there." Matt listened sympathetically as he recalled how Chad and Garth would have felt at this age.
"Go on, son," prompted Ben.
"Autumn had told me that she'd like to get to know me better. But at that point, I thought she was just trying to be nice. I remember giving it all up and going onto the other side of the deck, where no one was. I just sat there and wondered what my friends were doing. Then, all of a sudden, there was Autumn. Without saying a word, she sat down beside me. I thought she would try to put me on a guilt trip by asking me if I was enjoying her old party, but she didn't. Instead, she asked me about myself, about what

I was interested in. She knew all about music, the kind of music I like. Said she had some CD's she'd like for me to hear when we weren't surrounded by people who wouldn't appreciate them. She asked me about my friends and especially any girlfriends. I told her I didn't have a special girlfriend. Then she said that she supposed I'd never been *really* involved with a girl. She asked me that in a sorta teasing way. I said, 'No'. She touched me several times. It was real innocent, but I felt so excited by her touch. When she said she had to get back to her guests, I didn't want her to leave. She told me that I should come over some afternoon after school and we could play the CD's and get to know each other better. After a while, I went back inside. I didn't feel excluded anymore. Autumn insisted on fixing my plate for me; and when we sat down to eat, she sat beside me. Several times during the meal, she patted my leg. Then I was glad I came..." His voice trailed off.

"Sean, when did you next see Autumn?"

"Well, I saw her quite a few times after that...during the summer. She would be working in the yard or jog past the house. She did a lot of jogging you know."

"Did you take her up on her invitation to come over to her house?"

"Not right away. That happened after school started. One day I drove in from school just as she was jogging past my driveway. She stopped to speak to me. I remember she was so sweaty and breathless. She looked so natural. I was surprised that she stopped. I could hardly speak. She said why don't I come over for some Gatorade, and we'd listen to those CD's she'd told me about. So I did."

"Sean, when did you first have sex with her?" He wanted to make sure Sean understood his question.

"It was that day. We went into the back door of the house. I remember that she didn't say a word. She put on a CD and then went into the kitchen. I could hear her fixing us a drink. She came in and handed a glass to me and went over and turned the volume up on the player real loud. Then she came over and reached out for my hand and said...'Now we can hear it upstairs.' I used to dream about how that happened and what she had said. I thought it was just about the coolest thing I'd ever heard of." His eyes filled with tears again. "That was before I found out that my old man was sleeping with her."

Ben interrupted. "Sean, did you always go to Autumn's house?"

"Yes."

"How long did this continue? What I mean is, how long had you been having an affair with Autumn Hayes before her death?"

"I'm not sure. Several months."

"Well, we'll come back to that. Did you have any idea that your father was having an affair with Autumn before that day when you walked in on them?"

"No." Sean was beginning to shiver and more tears welled up in his eyes.

"Do you know of anyone else who might have been seeing Autumn?"

"No."

"Okay, just a couple of more questions here. On the day you made this discovery about your father, did *you* leave the house between the times you ran home from

Autumn's house until the next morning when her body was found?"

"No."

"Did your *father* leave the house between the times you ran home from Autumn's house until the next morning when her body was found?"

Anger crept across Sean's face. "I'd like to say yes. Just to get him into trouble. But he didn't. He didn't leave the house."

"And your *mother,* Sean. Did she leave the house between the times you ran from Autumn's house until the next morning when her body was found?"

"No, my mother was right here...fighting with him."

"Sean, I can't tell you how sorry I am that all this happened." Ben's voice was sincere. "If you remember anything that you think will be helpful in solving this case, please let me know. And Sean, if I can help you in any way, please don't hesitate to give me a call."

"Me, too, Sean," added Matt. "I have two sons of my own...a little older than you. I'd like to think that someone would be willing to help them if they needed help."

The men stood. Sean also arose clumsily. Ben extended a hand. "Take it easy now."

Matt stepped forward and instinctively clasped the young man around the shoulder and hugged him as he had so often comforted his sons when they felt such hopelessness. Sean responded awkwardly by patting Matt on the back.

A creaking sound caused the three to turn in the direction of the kitchen. Elizabeth Jeffreys was slipping stealthily into the room. Ben surmised that she had not been far away during the entire interview.

"Mrs. Jeffreys, Sean has been real helpful to me. I thank you and your husband for your time. And I thank you for allowing me to talk with Sean. Some kind of formal statement will be required at some time. I want to assure you again that I will keep it as relevant to this murder investigation as possible. Soon as the weather breaks, we'll talk further about the statement."

Matt and Ben moved toward the door. As they opened the door, they looked back to see Elizabeth Jeffreys sitting on the couch, rocking back and forth, her son cradled in her arms. John Jeffreys looked on from the kitchen, tears streaming down his face.

Ben and Matt slowly picked their way back to the road. The footprints they had left upon coming to the house had disappeared beneath a new powdering of snow.

"What about it, Matt?" Ben asked.

"What about what?"

"You know. What about that day at the barbecue? Did Autumn Hayes come on to you?"

Matt pondered the question silently. "You know, I guess she did. I remember that for a while she seemed to be especially interested in whether or not I was taken care of. But if I recall correctly, Ignatius and I were busy discussing this money that was to be allocated to NASA in Huntsville. We both thought that when Huntsville got the funds, we might be able to get some work from there. As I further recall, Jim Hayes was involved in the conversation, too. As a matter of fact, he's the one who told us about the funding. So Jim, Nate, and I spent a lot of time talking about that. I don't remember what happened to Autumn. All of a sudden she was just not there."

"Probably talking to Sean."

"Probably."

"Say, Matt," said Ben, "you think Ignatius might remember this long conversation you three had."

Matt stopped abruptly. "I don't know, Ben," said Matt harshly. "We could ask him. What am I? Your next suspect?"

"Hey, Matt, I have to check it all out. You know I don't think you could do something like this. But I have to check out everything...as much for your sake as for the investigation."

"Hey, thanks!"

"Suppose someone raised a question about you, or Nate, or anyone, and I hadn't checked them out. Wouldn't that look suspicious? Come on, Matt. You know how things like this can take a sudden twist. I've got to cover anything that could be questioned."

Matt appeared to be mollified. "I suppose so. It's just that I've been tramping around in this damned snow for days, just because you asked me to. Even that sounds suspicious now. Damn it, Ben. Did you have some ulterior motive for having me tag along like a hunting dog?"

"No ulterior motive. You're starting to sound paranoid." The men fell silent as they listened to the crunch of the snow. Finally they reached the road still hidden beneath the ice and frozen slush.

"Hey, buddy. Can I ask you a couple of questions?" said Ben.

"Are these questions coming from the Sheriff or from my friend?" Matt glared at Ben.

"Both. The questions are from your friend, who happens to be Sheriff."

"Okay. Shoot," Matt snapped.

"Did you have any other conversations, in person or by phone, with Autumn Hayes after the barbecue at her house last Fourth of July?"

"No, only an occasional greeting, as I have already told you."

"Have you met with Autumn Hayes at her house or at any other place...ever?"

"No!" Matt snarled.

"Do you have any other information that would help in the investigation of this case?"

Matt faltered. He thought of the dream. Would it help in the investigation of this case? Finally, Matt responded softly, "No, I know nothing more that would help in the investigation of your case, Ben."

The men stood speechlessly, their eyes locked in a tug of wills. The snow continued to fall peacefully. Finally Ben spoke. "Okay, Matt. I just had to ask. Hope you understand."

The men turned. Each headed in a different direction. Matt had not felt this depressed since his mother's death. How could this happen? How could he get sucked into this situation after he'd carefully built a life for himself that was supposed to be void of this kind of garbage? As he set about thoroughly berating himself for accompanying Ben on his investigation in the first place, an ear-splitting bellow resounded across the snow.

"Where the hell ya going? Matt, didn't you tell Ben about lunch? I been waiting for you." Ignatius' boisterous invitation was accompanied by the shrill sound of a dog yapping.

"Get back in here, Pete. You want to die of pneumonia? Come on, you two. I'm starved."

CHAPTER 20

Matt and Ben removed their coats and hung them on pegs in the hallway. Pete, still wearing a towel pinned across his body, yelped and jumped up and down as he frantically vied for the men's attention.

Ben sauntered into the kitchen followed by the hyper animal. Amid the clatter of dishes and pots, the Sheriff attempted to report the morning's disclosures to the cook. Ignatius listened intently, interjecting an occasional question. Matt stood before the blazing fire, studying the darting flames pensively. His silence appeared to go unnoticed.

Finally the three men sat down to a hearty lunch of coffee, black bean soup, saltine crackers, deliciously aged wheel cheese, and a dessert of buttermilk pie. Ignatius reached for a plastic cereal bowl that was setting beside his plate. As he lifted the bowl, Pete immediately took his place on the floor beside Ignatius' chair. He sat rigidly, eyes alert and ears poised. His tongue hung from the side of his mouth. His body quivered with anticipation as his friend filled the bowl with piping hot black bean soup, occasionally pausing to blow the entree vigorously. Finally the bowl was placed on the floor beside the chair. Pete's head jerked back and forth, and he growled at the hot contents as he impatiently attempted to eat his portion. Little conversation took place during the meal, but as the men pushed their chairs back and poured a second cup of coffee, the conversation turned once more to the Autumn Hayes investigation.

"Ignatius that was delicious soup. Where'd you learn to make that?" Ben inquired.

"It's a recipe I picked up when I lived out in Colorado. Glad you like it. It's a little spicy for Pete." Ignatius abruptly turned to Matt. "Okay, Matt, let's hear it. What the hell's eating you?"

Matt's eyes darted first from one man then the other. Finally he said, "Oh, nothing's wrong, Nate. It's just that Ben has decided to add me to his list of suspects in the Autumn Hayes murder investigation. That's all."

"Now, Matt, you know that's not so." Ben looked at Ignatius for understanding. "'Natius, Matt is mad because a couple of questions came up at the Jeffreys' interviews that I felt I needed to follow up on, for Matt's sake as well as for the sake of the investigation."

"Yeah, questions like did I ever have an affair with Autumn Hayes."

"*What?*" barked Ignatius. "Ben, what the hell's going on?"

Ben shook his head. "It didn't happen like he's making it sound," Ben protested. "When I was questioning Elizabeth about that barbecue, she indicated Autumn Hayes had paid more attention to Matt than was necessary for a hostess to pay. I felt as if I needed to cover that observation in case...suppose this thing went to court, Matt. Suppose Elizabeth made a statement like that on a witness stand. I'd look downright incompetent if I hadn't followed up on it. But, I have now, and I believe you. So what's the beef, Matthew?"

"I agree with Ben, Matt. Just because he has to check out statements, doesn't mean he's questioning your veracity. It's his job, for Pete's sake."

From his bed by the fireplace, the dog raised his head and barked in response to his name. The three men laughed, and the atmosphere of suspicion began to dissipate. The conversation quickly turned to a rigorous examination of the morning's findings. The conclusion was quickly reached that the Jeffreys family had been truly victimized by Autumn Hayes. It was agreed that the greatest sympathies lay with Sean, and there was much speculation as to any permanent scars that might be left.

"You know," said Ignatius, "one tends to think in terms of young girls being seduced. Little or no consideration is given to the fact that young boys can be victimized, too."

"Yes, that's true," replied Matt. "I have to admit that as a father of two sons, I never thought of an older woman taking advantage of them. I was really naive."

"You know what really gets me?" added Ben. "It's that this woman's violations were hardly noticed. And when they were, it was after the fact. She was like an old rat in a barn...she knew where all the holes were."

"Well, I feel sorry for Elizabeth Jeffreys," Matt said. You know it's going to be up to her to put her family back together. That is, if it can be put back together."

"I feel the same way about Elizabeth. It sounds to me like she was raising two boys," declared Ignatius.

"John Jeffreys ain't got a lick of sense," declared Ben.

"Say, Ben," said Matt, "Do you really think that Elizabeth dismissed Autumn's attention to John as just an ego trip for her husband?"

"I don't know, Matthew. Right now, I'm willing to give her the benefit of the doubt. If for no other reason, I have a feeling there's something else. Something I'm missing in this whole investigation. At first, I thought it was Jim Hayes. I was sure that when he showed up, there would be answers. Then when he turns up dead...well, the feeling hasn't gone away. I think there's something I ain't picked up on. Frankly, it's driving me nuts." He stood and stretched. "I guess I'd better get moving, or I'll fall asleep after that tasty hot meal. Think I'll just go on back to the office and look over my notes and the evidence again."

As he moved toward the hallway, Ignatius inquired, "Ben, I been wanting to ask you...have you had a chance to find out about Pete? What's gonna happen to him?"

"Oh, yeah, 'Natius, I meant to tell you. When I talked to Grady Hayes down in Austin, he said he didn't care anything about the dog. As far as he was concerned, you can have him."

"Great, Ben! Thanks. Hear that, Pete? No more stupid haircuts. You can live like a dog now." Pete merely grunted and stretched in his sleep.

As Ben pulled on his coat, he said, "Thanks again, Matt, for going with me to talk with your neighbors. No hard feelings?"

"No hard feelings, Ben. Keep in touch."

"Sure thing."

"And thanks for the lunch, 'Natius."

"Any time, Ben."

The doors blew shut and Ben disappeared into a flurry of snow. Ignatius turned to face Matt. "All right, let's have it. There's more to this than your being questioned about an affair with Autumn Hayes. Let's have it."

"It's that dream again Nate. When Ben was questioning me about Autumn, he also asked if I knew anything else that would help him in the investigation of this case."

"And you thought of that dream? Matt, there's no way that dream could help in the investigation of this case. In fact, it could lead Ben away from the truth if he got sidetracked by it. You did absolutely the right thing by not mentioning it."

"I guess you're right. It's just that I felt so evasive. And he appeared to be suspicious."

"Well, the sooner you put that dream out of your mind, the better off you'll be. How about a game of pool?"

"Hey, sounds great."

The drive back into Winchester was slow and tedious. Ben pulled onto Tenn. Highway 50. The sounds of winter treachery invaded the vehicle. Fine sleet pelted against the metal and glass of the windshield. The defroster roared as it gushed hot air against the window. Ice melted only to be quickly frozen again. Windshield wipers screeched and groaned as they struggled to clear a view of the snow-covered roads. Ruts that were cut earlier in the icy roads were now filled with fresh snow and frozen slush.

The tires crunched as they searched for a path. There were times when Ben could only hope that the car was still on the highway. So great was the concentration required to make the drive back into town that Ben was forced to push aside thoughts of the investigation.

As the patrol car reached the bridge over Dry Creek, Ben uttered a little prayer and cautiously pressed the accelerator. The car lunged forward onto the icy structure. Little benefit remained from the salting that had been done hours earlier, and there were no tracks on the bridge to provide a path. As he glanced over the guard rail into the blackness beneath the bridge, he thought of the summer hours he had spent fishing these waters with his friends. He tried to remember how it felt as the hot sun beat down upon him and his arms and neck stung from its burn. Finally, he reached the town-side of the bridge. The car advanced slowly up the hill and into town. He turned right and made his way toward Second Ave. NW.

The vacant streets made it unnecessary for him to stop at the four-way signs. He was, however, surprised to see a tan Cutlass Olds parked in front of Golden Leaves Bookstore. He pulled his vehicle in behind the Olds, turned up his coat collar, and stepped out into the snow. He cautiously stepped up where he thought the sidewalk should be and made his way toward the bookstore. The rectangular panes of glass in the storefront were covered with condensation. He strained to identify the store's occupant. Her gray hair was pulled back so severely that her eyes seemed to bulge. It was twisted upward into a bun and held in place with a large brown plastic hair pin. The woman huddled inside a light green hand-knitted sweater that was embroidered with pink and yellow rosebuds. Her hands, tipped with mauve nail polish, held a book at arms' length. She sat behind a large antique school teacher's desk. Ben tapped the window and lifted a gloved hand in greeting to the woman. She squinted and peered at him over half-glasses. Her expression remained unchanged as Ben opened the door to the bookstore.

"Hey, Mrs. Ernestine. I'm going next door. Want anything?"

"Coffee...black."

Ben closed the door and continued the few steps next door to the Hiatus. The cafe was empty, except for Dolores, whose eyes were fixed on a television set. She was absorbed in a steamy scene of an afternoon soap opera.

"Hi, Sheriff. Can I help you?" she said, never taking her eyes off the shirtless man who was gently coaxing a reluctant young woman toward the open door of a bedroom.

"Two large coffees...black, Dolores."

The distracted waitress poured the coffee into styrofoam cups, placed plastic covers on them, and set them on the counter without ever taking her eyes off the screen. Ben laid two bills on the counter.

"Keep the change, Dolores."

"Thanks, Sheriff."

Ben balanced the cups carefully and slowly made his way back to Golden Leaves Bookstore. He backed into the store and carefully set the steaming cups on the desk.

"Here you go, Mrs. Ernestine."

Mrs. Ernestine Kirkland tucked a crocheted bookmark between the pages of the book she was reading and carefully set it aside. Then she removed her glasses and placed them upon the book. Opening a drawer of the desk, she took out a tin container which was printed with "English Biscuits...London's Finest." She opened the tin and extended it to Ben. He removed a biscuit, which he popped into his mouth and consumed in one bite. Nodding his approval, he helped himself to three more.

"Good cookies, Mrs. Ernestine." Mrs. Ernestine frowned but said nothing.

Mrs. Ernestine Kirkland, better known as simply Mrs. Ernestine, had been Ben's high school English teacher and confidant. Ben had enjoyed Mrs. Ernestine's classes. She had a captivating way of making classic books and stories come alive, even for a mediocre English student like Ben. But most of all Ben appreciated Mrs. Ernestine because she was always there. Even before Ben reached high school, he remembered seeing Mrs. Ernestine downtown, in the grocery store, at church. It just seemed that all his life Mrs. Ernestine had lived there in Winchester. She seemed to be ageless. In his earliest recollection, Mrs. Ernestine had appeared to be an elderly, gray-haired, wrinkled lady, and she retained that appearance today. When Ben had a problem as a student, he sought out the town epic, the mother confessor, the local sage to give him comfort and succor. Mrs. Ernestine was all of those and then some. She seldom gave advice, but it seemed to Ben that when he left her room he always knew what to do. So when Mrs. Ernestine retired from teaching and opened Golden Leaves Bookstore, she merely moved her sessions from classroom to store. Ben and many other former students found her quiet and reassuring disposition still nurturing to them.

"So, Benjamin, how are you doing today?" her soft voice asked as she took a wee bite of her biscuit.

Without going into details that would betray confidences or disclose vital evidence, Ben told Mrs. Ernestine about the murder of Autumn Hayes and the discovery of her husband's body. He told her about the difficulty in questioning neighbors who had been affected by the murder, and told her of how it had been necessary to question his friend. He also spoke of the strong feeling that he was overlooking something vital...something obvious. Finally, he told her that he wondered why he had ever run for Sheriff of Franklin County.

Mrs. Ernestine sipped her coffee slowly and took small bites of her biscuit. Throughout Ben's reporting, her expressions continuously portrayed genuine concern for her former student.

"You've done just fine, Ben. You've done the best you can, and everything is going to be all right." It didn't sound patronizing when Mrs. Ernestine said that. It just sounded reassuring.

Ben had confessed his dilemma and received absolution of his frustrations. He was suddenly reinvigorated. "Think I'll go on over to the office and look over my notes and check out the evidence again. Maybe I'll spot something I've overlooked."

"You do that now, Ben."

As the bell on the store door signaled Ben's departure, Mrs. Ernestine replaced the lid on the biscuit tin and returned it to the desk drawer. Then, extending her book to arms' length, she snuggled down into her green sweater and began to read.

CHAPTER 21

Ben pulled his patrol car into a parking space behind the familiar red Ford Taurus. As a point of identification, he noted the damaged rear fender and the orange and white plaque displayed in the back window of the car that read, "God Must Have Been a U. T. Fan...He Painted the Sunset Orange." Ben had often wondered how his life would have been different if he had been able to play football for the University of Tennessee or even for the University of Alabama. Perhaps he, too, could have gone on to become another football coach from Franklin County in the likes of Johnny Majors and Phil Fulmer.

He thought back to his senior year in high school and how elated he felt upon being offered football scholarships from both the University of Alabama and the University of Tennessee. He remembered how proud his father had been. His dad had called relatives to share the magnificent news that the name Day would soon blare from television sets across the nation as his son returned punts, scored touchdowns, and made record-breaking runs. He remembered how, as a high school senior, he'd caught a pass and scored the winning touchdown in the game against Fayetteville that won the Conference Championship for Franklin County. He also remembered how he'd busted his knee in the process, costing him a scholarship to play football and the opportunity to go to college.

Dismissing thoughts from the past, Ben smacked the dented rear of the Taurus with his gloved hand, causing a small avalanche of snow to swoosh to the ground. Instinctively, he picked his way to the entrance of the station and welcomed the warm air that greeted him as he opened the door. A cursory surveillance of the glass-enclosed office told him that Penny was attacking her duties as the only office clerk. Her red acrylic nails mercilessly pounded the keys of a word processor that was trying to hide under copious papers on her desk. A burning cigarette smoldered in an ashtray awaiting an opportunity to ignite a carelessly placed document.

Ben took a deep breath and opened the door to the office. Penny's mouth began to move simultaneously with the click of the opening door.

"Sheriff, where have you been? I've been trying to reach you all morning. Don't you ever listen to your car radio? Suppose there was an emergency--"

"There is an emergency, Penny. Someone's been murdered. And that's where I've been, investigating this murder."

Ben displayed a grin that served only to kindle Penny's anger. He looked down into the ashtray at the source of the smoke...half a cigarette and an unbroken ash that had grown to the length of the filter.

"Don't you ever smoke these things? What do you do...just burn them?" Ben vigorously waved his hand in front of his face.

Penny ignored his comments, waving papers at him. "Messages...more messages. All about Autumn Hayes. I don't know anything about your case, Sheriff. How am I supposed to answer all these questions?"

"You're doing a real good job. I tell you what, Penny," Ben said, reaching into his pocket and leveling a crumpled piece of paper at her. "I have some information you can use in answering these inquiries. Here's the name of Jim Hayes' father. Lives in Austin, Texas. He'll be taking care of all the arrangements for Jim Hayes, depending upon the weather, of course. Direct some of these inquiries to him."

"And what about Autumn? Most of the calls are about her. And I'll tell you something else. A lot of these calls are just out of curiosity, but *now* I'm getting some that are downright nasty. Seems like sweet little Autumn wasn't always so sweet after all. So, what about the arrangements for her?"

"Grady Hayes will more than likely be taking care of her, too. Unless someone here has some information about Autumn's sister." He stared at the messages Penny had handed him. "Get me the names of the folks making the 'nasty' calls?"

"Yeah, it's all there. Got nothing about a sister, though. The way I see it, your biggest headache is the District Attorney. He wants to talk to you *yesterday*. He's already chewed me up and spit me out two or three times. I done told him I'm not in his dag-gone courtroom and to get off my case. I'm in no mood for him, Sheriff. I'm telling you."

Ben chuckled and said, "Penny, I just love it when you lay down the law."

"Yeah, and you just gonna *love* what else I got to say, Sheriff. The newspaper is your next biggest headache. This new guy over at the *Winchester News* has been calling me every hour on the hour. First off he asks to talk to you and then he starts asking *me* all these questions. I've told him and told him I don't know anything, and if I did I certainly ain't gonna share it with some little squirt tail who ain't got no manners. He told me that was called 'getting the facts'. I told him it was called 'harassment'. Ain't that called harassment, Sheriff?'

"No, Penny," Ben answered, continuing the banter, "that's called a newspaperman doing his job."

"Sheriff, why can't you take some of these calls?"

Ben shuffled through the messages, quickly perusing each one. He handed them back to Penny. "I can't return all these telephone calls, Penny. It's my job to solve a murder. It's your job to tend to the phone." Ben was already headed toward the door.

"But what about the D.A.? What about the guy from the *News*?" Penny was virtually shouting in an effort to thwart Ben's exit.

As Ben pushed open the door and stepped into the hall, Penny's voice was joined with that of yet another detractor. Dexter appeared from the cell-block area, and his shrill voice merged with the clamor of the debate. With unabated speed, Ben continued down the hall in the direction of the morgue...Dexter clipped along at his heels and waved a copy of the *Winchester News*.

"Sheriff, Penny is right. This is bad...real bad. It's all in the paper here. Have you read it? Listen to this."

Ben never missed a step in his jaunt down the hall. "No, Dexter. I haven't read it. I been too damned busy trying to solve this murder. It's my job to solve this case, and the *News* has to write about it. What do you expect? It's a murder."

"But, Sheriff, just listen to this...'found dead in her backyard...wound to back of her head...J. R. Hayes frozen to death...Murfreesboro...next of kin'--"

"Jim Hayes is Murfreesboro's headache now. They'll be sending the body to his father in Texas."

"But that part about the **back** of the head is **wrong**, anyway. Then it says, 'continues to explore all possible leads'..."

Ben's hand hit the swinging doors forcefully, as he abruptly entered the morgue. The doors swung back and smacked Dexter, who was continuing to detail the reporter's account from behind the newspaper.

"Hey, Sheriff," Doc Turner said.

"Hey Doc, just thought I'd stop by and see what you're up to."

"Nothing really. Just piddling around. Trying to get things squared away. Hope to get home before dark. Roads really get bad when the sun goes down."

"That they do. Anything new, Doc?"

"No...nothing new. Think you'll be able to make more sense out of my findings now. Got my notes all organized and my report typed up. Penny helped. She's a pistol."

"That she is," agreed Ben.

"Well, anyway, here it is." Doc Turner handed Ben several folders. One was filled with neatly typed pages of information, others were filled with photographs.

"Thanks, Doc. This will really help. You work real fast."

"Well, I'm not all that busy. We don't get a lot of murders in Franklin County...thank goodness."

"I've finished talking to the neighbors. With the information I got from them and your report, I hope I'll come up with some ideas. I plan to stay here tonight and really try to pull the thing together. There's one more thing, Doc. You think I could have another look at the body?"

A scurrying sound was heard from the back of the room. The two men turned to see the doors swing closed behind Dexter. They laughed.

"Sure, Sheriff. Looking for anything in particular?"

"I wish I was. I just got this feeling that I've overlooked something. Ever have that before?"

"Yeah. Well, come on over here." Removing a key from his pocket, he unlocked a large metal door. He reached into the dark hole and rolled out a slab on which lay the body of Autumn Hayes. "I'm through with her. She's all ready to go when the family wants her."

Ben moved close to the lifeless body. He bent his head toward her still face. Dark hair...almost black...spilled over the white cover. She wore no make-up, of course. Her face had a deep golden, salubrious tan that extended down her throat and onto her shoulders and arms. The hideous wound on the top of her head had done massive damage. Yet, her beauty was still apparent. Ben stared hard at the wound that had drained the life out of Autumn Hayes. He looked next at her hands that also revealed a smooth, flawless tan. They had been gracefully crossed atop the cover on her chest. Long, thin fingers tapered to end with well-manicured, bright red nails. Ben noticed a small bump on the side of the middle finger of her right hand. It had the appearance of a small callus. He slipped the cover down, exposing the full bosom tipped with large, dark brown nipples. He was surprised to see that the tan spread evenly over her entire torso. Only a small patch of white skin in the v-shape of a bikini strap could be seen across the pubic area. His eyes followed the tan down her legs and to her feet. Red polish on her toenails matched that on her fingernails. She was obviously impeccably groomed. Ben pulled the cover over the body. Doctor Taylor returned the slab to the vault and slammed the door noisily. As he locked the metal door and returned the key to his pocket, he laughed nervously, "Just so she won't go anywhere." He patted the pocket that now housed the key.

"Doc, lemme ask you a few questions."

"Sure. Shoot."

"Did she have any make-up on when she was brought in here?"

"Nope. No make-up. What you getting at?"

"Well, it's just that I'd suspect someone like Autumn Hayes to use at least a little bit of make-up if she'd expected company. I don't understand this suntan, Doc. How'd she get that kind of a tan in the winter?"

"Easy. They got tanning beds at most every beauty parlor now. Folks can spend a few minutes a week and have a tan all winter. Strip down naked and you can actually tan your hide. Lot of medical concern about the effects of tanning beds though. But that's got nothing to do with this case."

"I noticed that Autumn Hayes had a callus on the middle finger of her right hand. Any idea what might have caused that?"

"Sure do. Comes from gripping your pen or pencil too tight. My wife has a big one on her middle finger. She's a teacher, you know, and checks a lot of papers."

"Just one other question, Doc. According to one of the people I interviewed this morning, Autumn Hayes had sex the day before she died. Did your tests substantiate that claim?"

"Nope. No sign of that. Of course, if it were the day before, she could have bathed, douched. She seemed to be a well-groomed person. It's right in the report there, Sheriff. Any more questions?"

"How about letting me have the box containing the clothes and other evidence found at the crime scene?"

The doctor walked to the back of the room and returned carrying a large cardboard box with the name HAYES written in big letters on the side. Attached to the top of the box was a form giving the name of victim, case number, investigating officers, date and location of crime and a list of the contents of the box.

"Anything else, Sheriff?"

"I'm sure there will be when I read these reports and look over this evidence again. Much obliged, Doc. I hope Penny didn't give you a real hard time."

"Heck, no. That little ol' gal is the only ray of sunshine around this gloomy place." As Ben walked out of the morgue, he shook his head and laughed.

When Ben returned to the office, Penny had left for the day. Sitting behind her desk was Dexter, ever vigilant. Ben realized that the office seemed especially quiet without Penny's prattle and the ringing of the telephone. Dexter attempted to fill the void of sound.

"Sheriff, now you just go on and do whatever you got to do. I'll take care of this pesky telephone. Don't expect you'll get too many calls, however. *Winchester News* office is closed. And you know that the D.A.'s gone home. Folks at home now eating supper. I think things are gonna settle down and get real quiet now..." He rambled on as he lifted his feet up on the desk, leaned back, and locked his hands behind his head.

Ben took his place behind his seldom-occupied desk. He set the large box containing evidence on the floor. Placing the folders squarely in the center of the desk, he opened the top one. It contained large black and white photographs of the crime scene. Ben meticulously arranged them on his desktop. Using a magnifying glass, he scrutinized each picture. Yielding to curiosity, Dexter solemnly joined Ben as he conducted this examination. There were shots of the body taken from different angles. The face of Autumn Hayes was almost obscured by snow and hair that was matted with blood and tissue from the massive wound. Her body appeared to be relaxed...asleep...as it stretched out upon the snow. There were pictures of the wood that was scattered about and the large jagged rock that was covered with blood. The rock had been circled in red. There were pictures of the leather log carrier. There were pictures of the crime scene taken from the house, and pictures of the house taken from the crime scene.

"Huh," grunted Ben. As he rose into an upright position, his head bumped against Dexter, who was bending over Ben, intently engrossed in the pictures that were spread upon the desk.

"Oops. Sorry, Sheriff. I think that there is my boot," he said, pointing to an intruding black boot in one of the photographs.

"Yeah, Dexter. I was wondering whose boot that was. Who's keeping an eye on the Hayes neighborhood?"

"Antonio is out there tonight."

"Well...just so you got someone there all the time. I don't want any suspects packing up their car and pulling out in the middle of the night."

"I don't think they would do that in this weather, Sheriff."

"Well, who would have thought that Jim Hayes would have tried a stunt like driving all the way from Nashville to Winchester in a blizzard? I want you to keep that place covered, Dexter," Ben said firmly.

"Right, Sheriff...no sweat."

Ben collected the pictures of the crime scene and placed them back in the folder labeled CRIME SCENE PHOTOS. Setting it aside, he reached for the next folder.

The second folder contained autopsy photographs taken by Doc Turner. Following his established routine, Ben arranged these photographs on his desk and proceeded to examine each one. Dexter feigned indifference and found something to do at the other desk. In examining these photographs, Ben moved far more expeditiously than he had with the previous ones. Finally, he collected the pictures and returned them to the folder labeled LAB PHOTOS.

Next, Ben opened the folder that contained Doc Turner's written report so neatly typed by Penny. He read carefully each observation and finding reported by the doctor. Doc had also included a fax from the Huntsville, Alabama Doppler Radar Weather Center that gave the time it started snowing in the Winchester Area. Ben noted this time. He then reread the report and placed it back in the appropriated folder.

Next, Ben turned to his notes on the investigation and interviews with the neighbors. His notes were neither as well organized nor as neat as Doc's. His review began with his arrival at the crime scene and ended with the interview of Sean Jeffreys. Ben had chosen not to make written notes on his questions about Autumn's flirtation with Matt. Nothing jumped out at him. But there still remained the feeling of having overlooked something.

Ben stood up and stretched back, gently pounding his lower back with his fists. Dexter looked up from a copy of the *Winchester News* and paused in his third reading of the Hayes investigation. He was delighted to discover that his name had been listed as a member of the "investigative team".

"You know Sheriff that young man did a pretty good job of reporting on the Hayes case. After all we all had to experience the *first time*...the first time to ride a bicycle, the first time to drive a car, the first time to investigate a murder, and the first time to write a newspaper article about a murder. Yes sir, for his first try, he done a pretty good job." Dexter noticed the dark circles under Ben's eyes that became pronounced when he was fatigued. "Say, why don't you call it a day?"

"Not yet, Deputy."

Dexter grinned. He liked it when Ben called him Deputy. "Well, how about a cup of coffee then?"

"Sounds good. Black." Ben bent over, lifted the large cardboard box, and set it up on the desk. He began to remove the contents and place them on the desk. Each item was bagged separately and labeled accordingly. There was a blue denim jacket with the collar and shoulder soaked with a dark stain. Size ten. A pair of faded Levi jeans, size eight, spattered with a dark stain. A pair of well-worn, high-heel black boots, size six and a half. He noticed that the back side of the right boot was scuffed and in need of a good polish. The outside of the heel was badly worn. He also found a pair of leather gloves. The fingers of the right glove were considerably more worn than the fingers of the left glove. Next was an oak-handled leather log carrier. This, too, showed a smattering of dark stain. The sixth item was a 22-pound, jagged rock. The rock was heavily stained with blood, type O Positive. What appeared to be dry leaves and mud were stuck to one side of the rock. There was also a black leather belt trimmed with silver discs and turquoise-colored stones and a gray sweatshirt, large, embossed with bold pink letters that read, "Florida is for Lovers." The right side of the neck of the shirt was soaked with a dark stain. Spattering extended down the front. Next was a pair of gray woolen socks. They looked to be brand new. One size fits all. Conspicuously absent from the box were any underclothes.

Ben studied each item carefully. His big fingers carefully touched and explored each object. He inspected any typical or atypical aspect of every article. He tried to visualize Autumn as she put on each item of clothing. What would she put on first...second...next? How would she carry the log basket? Did she see the murderer? How did she react? Then he stopped abruptly. He frantically opened the folder containing the crime scene photos. He leafed through them quickly and removed several pictures from the group. He examined the boots, and then looked at the picture of Autumn stretched so peacefully on the ground. He snatched the folder that contained the lab photos. Hurriedly, he grabbed the picture of Autumn lying with her hands crossed gracefully upon the white cover. He reached for a magnifying glass and squinted at an enlarged section of the photo. He seized the boot again. Of course! Hastily, Ben began to replace each item of evidence in the box. As he worked he began to yell.

"Dexter...Dexter...Where are you? Hey Deputy!"

Dexter had taken advantage of Ben's absorption in his work to step into the snack area and pass around his copy of the *Winchester News* to other officers on duty. When he heard the first bellow from the Sheriff, he'd dropped his Sundrop can, snatched the paper from a fellow officer's hands, and sprinted toward the front office.

"Right here. What can I do for you?"

"What can you do for me? Hell, Deputy, I think I got this thing figured. Hot damn!" Ben was out of his seat, rushing toward the middle of the room. He grabbed Dexter by the arms and whirled him around in square-dance fashion. Then he soloed a jig and continued to shout. "Hot damn! You ain't such a smarty, Miz Autumn Hayes!"

Upon hearing the commotion, officers from the snack room clamored into the office. Ben slapped them on the back and laughed and swore. Then he sped back to his desk and grabbed for the phone.

"Dexter, I want you, Neil, and Scott to go with me out to the Hayes place. Antonio is already there. Call him and tell him we're coming. Gotta call Matthew and 'Natius." Ben snatched up the telephone. There was silence.

"What the hell's the matter with the telephone?"

"Sheriff," muttered Dexter, afraid that retribution would be visited on the messenger, "all the telephone lines are out in Winchester. Don't know how it is out thatta way. But here they're as dead as a doornail."

CHAPTER 22

Bent against the wind, Matt looked like an Arctic explorer as he made his way back up the hill to his place. Sleet and snow pelted his face mercilessly. The flashlight was of little use in locating the sinuous road up the hill, and Matt was struck again by the ineffable stillness of the woods.

When he reached his log house, Matt made no attempt to locate the path to his front door. He decided to simply tramp in the general direction of his place. Aiming the flashlight toward his house, he illuminated the yard and the front of the dwelling. As the shaft of light scanned the front window, four portentous yellow eyes glared out at him. Their demonic gleam explained why even today people avoid cats. Matt, however, welcomed the ocular reflections peering at him through the darkness and used them as a beacon to reach his house.

When he reached the porch of his log house, he unzipped the pocket of his parka and retrieved a key. His gloved hand awkwardly unlocked the door. As he stepped into the sanctuary of his home, Matt immediately felt the affectionate greeting of Aslan and Spencer as they nuzzled him and rubbed against his ankles. When Matt removed his parka and gloves and shook away the wet snow and melting ice, he heard the thumping of a hasty cat retreat as they galloped into the vacuous darkness. Matt's hand felt along the wall beside the door. Flipping the light switch, he illuminated the room. A great sense of relief swept over him. He spied the two cats sitting on the sofa, indignantly removing the wet snow and ice from their coats.

"Sorry fellows. That was a mean trick after you gave me such a friendly greeting. How about some dinner? How does mixed grill sound?" The cats ignored Matt's attempts to appease them and continued to meticulously lick their paws and wipe them across their faces. Then as Matt headed toward the kitchen, Aslan and Spencer sped past him and perched on the counter.

The cats settled on a salmon dinner for their meal. Matt sipped strong, dark coffee and watched as they polished their plates contentedly. The house was silent. Occasionally, the wail of the winds penetrated the log walls. An anomalous tapping could be heard as sleet and snow attacked the window and threatened the security of the snug kitchen. Matt arose and clicked a switch that lighted the wintry yard. Naked, white trees lifted their arms upward and waved them balefully. Throughout the woods, pops or cracks could be heard as limbs laden with ice plummeted to the ground. The visual and sound effects of the winter stage produced the illusion of a spectral army marching menacingly toward the window. The deck steps were covered with snow, and four-foot-high drifts obscured the handrail. A blast of wind lifted some snow and it spiraled across the backyard like a whirling dervish. A tattered plastic bird feeder swung recklessly from the bare branch of a dormant dogwood tree. The empty ornament attested to the winter plight of the birds. The sliding glass door overlooking the woods clattered and trembled. Matt shuddered at the moan of the wind. He felt that his sanctuary was being besieged.

Finally Matt reached for a cord that hung beside the door. Pulling the thin rope, he hastily shut out the harsh view. He lifted his coffee mug and walked toward his study. The wind followed him from room to room. Its mournful wail was inescapable. Matt had never experienced such a feeling of loneliness and dread. It had become apparent to him that he shared Ben's feeling that they were overlooking something pertinent.

"I'm too damned close to this thing," he said aloud. His loud declaration appeared to go unnoticed by the cats that joined him as he walked through the house.

What Matt needed was an objective ear...someone completely detached from the circumstances. Caryn! Caryn, who would listen and neither reprimand nor judge. What time is it? Eight-thirty here, nine-thirty there. Oh, why not?

Ring, ring...five rings. Then, "Hello," muttered a soft, sleepy voice.

"Caryn?...Matt."

"Why Matt, who else?"

"I woke you up," Matt stated.

"What a nice thing to wake up to. Tell me about the turbulent times in Tennessee."

Matt heard a faint rustling. He imagined Caryn pushing herself into a sitting position. He brought her up to date on the investigation, and he thanked her again for her background information on Autumn Hayes.

"Poor Matt, you've been a busy boy. I would suggest that your friend, Ben, should be most appreciative of you and Ignatius. It helps to bounce ideas off people who have no responsibility in the matter."

"Yeah, like I bounce ideas off you."

"Yes...or whatever."

Matt laughed. "By the way, Caryn this guy Joseph Dixson...the one Autumn was attracted to at Computech. Did you ever find out what his wife's name was?"

"Yes, I did. Hope. Hope Henley Dixson."

"Hmmm..."

"Matt," Caryn interrupted Matt's thoughts. "I was thinking the other day about how nice it would be to actually see yo--"

The telephone issued a series of crackles and whistles. Matt yanked the receiver from his ear. The cats dashed from the study. The static was followed by total silence.

"Damn," swore Matt, "the telephone's out." Now Matt really felt like a prisoner in a glacial prison.

Ben accompanied by three other officers, pulled on their coats and gloves and beat a hasty exit from the office into the night. The wind had subsided, and the clouds parted enough to reveal a gigantic yellow moon. Its gentle radiance was reflected in the snow that covered the streets and light posts. On the Victorian storefronts, obsolescent colors occasionally penetrated the winter covering. An astounding stillness lay upon the village. Ben was reminded of a scene from a science fiction movie in which the population fled the invasion of an alien army. The four men stuffed themselves into the patrol car. Ben took the seat beside Scott, the self-appointed driver. Scott flipped the switch that activated the blue lights and started the car.

"Forget the lights, Scottie, I don't think anyone will get in our way. Besides, I don't want to advertise our arrival. Take her slow and quiet," instructed Ben.

"Don't you worry Sheriff, Scott's real good at driving in this snow. He was born up in Washington, D. C.," Dexter's reassuring voice came from the back seat. "And he also knows these roads like a taxi cab driver." Ben groaned when the rear end of the car fish-tailed as it turned the corner onto Cedar Street.

"Take it easy now," Ben cautioned. He curled his toes and braced his feet against the floorboard.

Matt peeled away his clothing, leaving on only his long winter underwear. Clicking the light switch, the room plunged into darkness. He yanked the cord of the bedroom curtain, exposing the clearing in the back of his house. Matt then crawled under his eider down comforter, supported his head with two large feather pillows, and gazed at the frozen wonderland.

Two comforting cats snuggled amongst the folds of the quilt. The howling winds subsided. There was only a gentle breeze now that slowly moved the clouds across the sky. Straight ahead of him, between two tree trunks, the moon was just appearing, very large and golden. The world seemed so still. Matt felt that he was the only person alive. He began to shiver. Then, from the corner of the clearing, a movement could be detected beneath the snow. Mounds of snow, much like dirt mounds created by a mole, moved in a zig-zag fashion toward the house. Contours of subterranean creatures could be seen pushing the mounds forward, ever closer. A glow radiated from the mounds as they quickly grew in length. It was a heinous blood-red glow that defiled the spotless white blanket of snow.

From within the woods there arose the distinct, continuous patter of hoofs against frozen snow. Matt was terrified. His eyes fixed in a rigid stare, dreading what horror might emerge from the trees. Suddenly, a dreadful sight sprang upon the scene. A white deer, so white that the snow was colorful by comparison, vaulted into the clearing. It was very large, and its antlers shone like something afire. His rack emitted a phosphorescent glow, and a bluish green flame spewed forth from its mouth. His savage eyes were red and piercing. They were directed toward the house...and Matt. Behind the fiendish animal plodded two cadaverous fawns struggling pitifully to maintain their footing.

Seated in a saddle on the back of the gigantic deer was a woman. Autumn Hayes. She was wearing a white shroud that twisted and flew as the wild beast bucked and reared. Her arms were milk white, and they waved and thrashed about as she struggled to stay on the back of her mount. Long red nails protruded from her fingers like scarlet stilettos. Her face was deathly pale, except for a bright red iridescent mouth that turned up into a hideous, diabolical smile. Her eyes revealed no white, only the dark chocolate irises flashed in the moonlight as they searched the clearing. Her eyes eventually met Matt's. Curling her fingers into a claw-like position, she made maniacal slashing gestures toward him. The deer reared and lunged in the direction of the window.

The mounds that now zigzagged across the clearing suddenly ruptured. Hundreds of little gray creatures spewed forth and crawled about. Their eyes were blood red, their reflection radiated on the snow. They were repugnant earthworms...wiggling, crawling, moving ever closer to the bedroom window. Matt could hear a sucking sound as they attached themselves and then crawled up the side of the log house. They were on the window ledge, and stuck on the window. Their eyes glowed and they wiggled and squirmed. Matt heard a crunching sound, and he realized that they were gnawing. Matt could hear them gnawing at the window frame. The deer...the fiendish deer...reared and whinnied, throwing phosphorescent drool upon the glass. The mounted apparition tossed her head in a silent laugh and motioned the worms on. The two pitiful fawns shivered in the snow as earthworms crawled about their hoofs.

The gnawing of the wood intensified. Then, Matt heard a cracking, splintering sound. Suddenly, a gust of frigid air permeated the room, and shattered glass cascaded...almost in slow motion...to the floor. Scores of gray earthworms with red eyes spilled over the window sill and began to crawl toward the bed. Two frightened felines hunched their backs in horror.

"HELP!" screamed Matt, thrashing his arms in an effort to thwart the onslaught.

The cats yowled and hissed.

Matt battled to free himself from the bedding that bound him. He lashed and struck out at whatever held him. Arms...feet...struggled, flayed at the source of restraint. He tossed the comforter to the floor. Finally, he was loose. He threw his feet to the floor, only to snatch them up quickly as he remembered the earthworms.

A dream. Another damned dream! He covered his face with his hands and rubbed his eyes.

Then Matt flipped on the light. When he searched the room for the cats, Spencer could not be found. Aslan was perched on a high wardrobe, glaring down with a vengeful stare.

"Sorry, Old Buddy," Matt's voice was scratchy, almost unrecognizable. Aslan eyed him with renewed distrust. "Let's hope that this one doesn't happen, or your meal ticket's going to end up being committed. What would you have to say about that?"

Matt sat on his bed and listened to his heart pound and threaten to explode inside his chest. He shook violently, and his teeth chattered so hard that he thought they would crack.

Spencer's eyes peered out from beneath the chest. He slowly emerged and jumped up on the bed. Soon he was rubbing against Matt, an act of forgiveness and tolerance. Aslan remained on top of the wardrobe. Matt found the cat's adoration soothing, and soon he no longer shook. He began to piece together the events of the day, ending with his telephone call to Caryn that had been so abruptly terminated. Suddenly awareness set in. Of course! How could he have been so stupid?

"Yes!" cheered Matt. His fists shot upward in a gesture of victory. His feet hit the floor with a thud that sent Spencer scurrying back under the chest. Aslan arched his back and growled in disapproval at Matt's relapse.

"Of course, that's it! Of course..." Matt reached for the telephone and then dropped it quickly as he remembered the phone was dead. "Shit!"

He was throwing on clothes haphazardly while moving toward the front door.

"Got to find the man that Ben left to guard the neighborhood….the Hayes house? Got to find him."

The front door slammed. Two green eyes peeped anxiously from under the chest, and a dubious black cat emerged. Cautiously, he jumped on the bed and began to knead the feather comforter. Aslan cynically observed this action. Then he, too, leapt on the bed and curled himself among the soft folds of the eider down quilt.

CHAPTER 23

Ignatius reached for his pipe and began to fill it with his favorite blend that was sent to him from The Tobacco Shop in Nashville. The ritual of filling the pipe was as comforting to Ignatius as smoking it. So he never hurried, and his finest thinking was done while performing this task.

Pete recognized this practice as a prelude to sleep. He ambled to his bed, scratched the towel into a pile, turned three times, and lay down. He blinked his eyes sleepily as he watched Ignatius create clouds of smoke. Soon, his eyes remained shut.

Ignatius fed logs to the blazing fire, and the leaping flames made it unnecessary to turn on the lights. He directed a melancholy look at the photographs on the mantel. The green eyes seemed to smile at him, confirming a love that could not be obliterated by death. Ignatius smiled back. He studied the blaze pensively, reflecting on the day's events. He was relieved that his two friends had resolved their differences and thought how unfortunate it would be if Autumn Hayes were capable of weaving her web of discontent even from the grave.

Ignatius turned his attention to the dazzling landscape in his backyard. When Matt brought in logs from the deck, he had left the curtains open. Now, Ignatius could view a large orange moon and the dazzling icy spectacle its radiance produced. So peaceful a vista it was, it was unfathomable that such violence could have invaded their community. He pondered that one could be so unaware of what was going on next door. He considered how two personalities could be housed in the one body...one luscious body. One personality was socially acceptable; the other personality was vile and cunning. He wondered if all people actually possessed this kind of duplicity, with their choice of behavior determining if one is normal or abnormal.

Suddenly, a shadow of a person silhouetted against the snow moved slowly across the glass door. The palms of the hands pressed against the glass in an effort to maintain footing. With each step the snow crunched, the only sound breaking the frightful silence. An odious face pressed hard against the window. The distorted nose and mouth squirmed about, as wild eyes scanned the snug shelter inside. The stare fixed on an indeterminate object in the room. An unrelenting, macabre wail resounded across the snow. The figure was pounding frantically against the glass door. It rattled and shook. Ignatius feared that it would soon explode, admitting the mad person. He gasped and pushed his wheelchair into a dark corner of the room. The person was knocking and bellowing words that were incoherent. The cacophony of appalling sounds reached an incredible level. The hands found their way to the door handle.

"The door...the door...don't let the door be unlocked," whispered Ignatius. He reached for the phone to dial 911. A feeling of horror gripped him as he realized the line was out.

Pete was barking wildly and jumping at the door. He snarled and growled, pawing savagely at the floor around the door. The shadow grasped the handle and slowly pulled open the door. Pete retreated to the bed that offered him security. He dropped onto the towel and whined and shook.

A ghastly woman was in the room. Her hair was in wild disarray. She moved her lips savagely and issued a torrent of mindless babble. A sharp chin protruded below her toothless mouth, and spittle dropped onto her stained dress. She wore neither coat nor boots. She was dressed only in a dirty, wrinkled house dress and house slippers that were coated with ice and snow. Her eyes flashed wildly about the room. She didn't appear to see Ignatius. She continued her insane gibberish as she moved, hands extended, toward the fireplace.

Ignatius realized that she was going for Pete. Disregarding his own safety, he rammed his wheelchair forward, overturning a table and knocking a lamp to the floor. The horrible face turned abruptly, her crazed eyes glaring wildly at the distraction. With a maniacal shriek, she lunged for Ignatius. Powerful Amazon-like hands clutched his neck, squeezing the life out of him. The chair rolled back against the overturned table and turned over, spilling Ignatius to the floor. She straddled his chest. Breathe...try to breathe, Ignatius thought wildly. He realized that his labored breath was filled with smoke. Struggling, he managed to turn his head. His lit pipe had been placed on the table that was now overturned. The newspaper was burning. He couldn't breathe, and began to lose consciousness.

Then he heard voices. "Ignatius, you all right?"

"Nate, it's me. Can you hear me? It's me...Matt. Come on Ignatius. Can you hear me?"

"Hey 'Natius, listen up...it's Ben. Let's go. See if we can set him up...Got that fire out? Hey 'Natius...come on, buddy."

Hands slipped under Ignatius' arms, and he was lifted into his chair. He looked around the room. Ben and Matt were standing over him, concern etched on their faces. The glass door was wide open and the room was getting cold fast. A wretched-looking woman stood by the fireplace, her hands covering her face. She was whimpering pitifully. Dexter and Scott, looking prepared yet confused, stood on either side of her. Pete stood at her feet, sniffing her soggy slippers.

"Close the damned door," roared Ignatius. "I can't heat the whole county. How's Pete?"

"Pete's okay, Nate. The question is...how are you?" asked Matt.

"How am I?" he asked incredulously. "Oh, I'm just fine, Matt. Just fine. I'm sitting here in my own house, minding my own business, and some maniac busts in here and tries to kill me. But other than that, I'm all right. Who the hell is she, anyway? That woman's a lunatic!"

"Ignatius, let me introduce you to your neighbor...Ida Phillips," Ben said.

"Ida Phillips? Well, what the hell did she do this for? Is she completely insane?"

Pete stopped sniffing Ida's shoes. He began to bark and jump up on the pathetic woman. He dashed about her, yelping as he ran. Ida Phillips emitted a pitiful sob and removed her hands from her face. Dexter and Scott quickly grabbed her arms. She produced a mournful cry and began to struggle fiercely. Her strength almost exceeded that of the two officers. The dog began to bark, furniture toppled, and shrieks and cries pierced the air.

Suddenly from the doorway, a voice blared, "Leave her alone! Please leave her alone! She's like a little child. Leave her alone!" Jesse Phillips leaped into the room and rushed to his wife's side.

Dexter and Scott dropped their grasp on her arms and stepped away. Jesse cradled his wife in his arms, whispering softly to her. She slunk into the rocker. As if on cue, Pete jumped into her lap and began to lick her face lavishly. The despicable woman cradled the dog in her arms and began to rock.

"Baby...sweet Baby...I love you. Yes, Baby," she cooed.

Then suddenly the rocking became more vigorous, and a mournful voice crooned its dirge..."Like the faint dawn of the morning, Like the sweet freshness of dew, Comes the dear whisper of Jesus, Comforting tender and true...Whispering Hope...like the song of the angels..."

The men stared in morbid fascination. As Ida rocked Pete, Ben and Matt recognized the hymn that had played over and over when they interviewed Jesse. It was impossible to believe that this decrepit-looking woman could possess such strength as was evidenced by the ransacked room.

Ida Phillips suddenly stopped singing. The room was deathly still. Ignatius was amazed to see that Pete's eyes were actually closed. She had indeed rocked the animal to sleep. Jesse Phillips gently unfolded the arms that cuddled

Pete, and calmly eased the dog from her grasp. He handed the animal to Dexter, who in turn gave him to Ignatius. Jesse then unbuttoned his coat and removed a stuffed animal. It was a little stuffed white poodle with a red felt nose and black plastic eyes. Ida stirred. Jesse gently placed the stuffed toy in Ida's arms.

"Here you go, honey. Here's Baby," he said, tears streaming down his ruddy cheeks.

Jesse walked over to Ben. "She'll be all right now, Sheriff. She's okay when she has that toy. I fell asleep, and when I woke up, she was gone. I was afraid she was over here. She watched you leave the Jeffrey's' house today. When Ignatius came out to speak to you, she saw that dog run outside. She was sure it was her stuffed animal. I told her it wasn't. She wouldn't accept that." He nodded toward the stuffed dog. "I argued with her all day. Never could convince her. Me...I just got plum tuckered out. Fell asleep watching TV. I knew right off the bat she was over here. I'm so sorry, Ignatius. She's just like a little child."

"Mr. Phillips, I got to talk to you...tonight," Ben asserted. "You wanta talk here or at your place?"

"Oh, Sheriff, please, not tonight. You seen how she is--"

"No, Mr. Phillips," Ben's voice was stern. "We're gonna talk tonight."

Jesse Phillips' shoulders dropped in resignation. "Okay, Sheriff. Let me take Ida home. I've got a real strong sedative that the doctor gave me for when she's bad off. Guess this is the time to use it. But let's talk here. I don't want to take a chance of upsetting her again."

"Okay," said Ben. "Dexter...you, Scott, and Antonio go with the Phillipses. You think you can get her home, Mr. Phillips?"

"Yes," he answered. He bent over Ida, his sinewy arms gently lifting her languid form.

"Antonio, you and Scottie stay there with Mrs. Phillips, and Dexter, you come on back here with Mr. Phillips."

The men left through the front door. Flashlights in hand, Dexter led the way. Scott and Neil walked on either side of Jesse Phillips, ready to react should he slip on the ice. Antonio followed behind the entourage.

"Now," growled Ignatius, still gripping Pete in his lap, "to what do I owe the pleasure of your visit?"

Matt and Ben stared at each other questioningly. "Yeah, Ben, what are you doing here this time of night?"

"What are you doing here?" Ben returned.

"I came down looking for the officer you left to guard the Hayes place. My phone is out, and I thought he could get you on his car radio."

"Ben?" Ignatius pursued.

"I'm here because, when I started up the hill toward the Hayes place, I heard this gosh-awful scream and saw Matt running toward the back of your house."

"None of this explains why you two were out in the first place," Ignatius persisted.

Matt dropped into the rocker that Ida Phillips had vacated. "Tonight I talked with Caryn Shipley, before the telephone lines went out. It was mostly a personal conversation. But just before we were cut off, I asked her if she had been able to find out the name of Joe Dixson's wife.

You know the one who committed suicide. She told me that she had. Dixson's wife was Hope Henley Dixson. Right away, the name rang a bell. Then before I could collect my thoughts, the telephone went dead. I went to bed still having the conversation on my mind. I had a rough night. Lots of bad dreams and stuff." He cast a conspiratorial eye at Ignatius. "I suppose my subconscious must have been at work. Later, when I woke up, I remembered why I found the name so troubling. Hope...Whispering Hope. Remember, Ben? When we went to the Phillips' house, Ida Phillips kept playing the same gospel song over and over...Whispering Hope. And it was the same song she sang to Pete tonight. Remember? So I'm thinking that Ida Phillips' niece was named Hope. Hope Henley Dixson. Autumn Hayes was screwing around with the husband of Ida's niece. And because of the affair, Hope committed suicide.

"And remember the dog, Ben? Jesse Phillips told us that Ida gave her niece a little dog for Christmas, and she named it Baby? When Ida was rocking Pete tonight, what did she call him?"

"Baby," Ben answered.

"Autumn Hayes was having an affair with the husband of Ida's niece." Ignatius whistled loudly, "Ben, that surely gives you a prime suspect for the murder of Autumn Hayes. Wouldn't put it past Old Ida. Why, you saw how crazy she was tonight. She was strong as any two men I know."

Ben rubbed his chin and shook his head. "Good thinking, Matt. And I'll bet you're right about Hope Henley Dixson being Ida Phillips' niece. It'll be easy enough to check out. But I can't arrest her for the murder of Autumn Hayes."

Matt looked shocked. "Why not?"

"I can't arrest her for the murder of Autumn Hayes, because Autumn Hayes may not be dead."

Matt and Ignatius simply gawked at Ben incredulously. The room was silent except for the snap of the blazing logs. Ignatius' voice cracked as he whispered, "Ben, what are you doing up here tonight?"

CHAPTER 24

Ben's explanation was interrupted by the sound of footsteps on the front porch. "We're back, Sheriff," Dexter announced.

"Ida won't give them no trouble, Ben. She's worn down, and that sedative just knocked her right out. Ignatius, I can't tell you how sorry I am that this happened," Jesse Phillips apologized again. "I guess it's to the point that I can't take care of Ida no more. Lord knows I've tried, but she's stronger than I am. I'm gonna call her sisters today, and we'll try to figure out how to take care of her."

The lines etched on Jesse Phillips' face reflected the fatigue and defeat he felt at his failure to care for his wife. He collapsed into a chair, looking hopefully toward the three men for some sign of understanding.

Ben said, "Mr. Phillips, before you came in, I was getting ready to explain why I made this trip out here in the middle of the night. Under the circumstances, I now feel that what I have to say will affect you.

"You see, for days I have been investigating the murder of Autumn Hayes. Today, things took an interesting turn. When I went back to the office, I viewed the body and took a good look at all my evidence again. Then I began to pull things together. We've got a murder here but, it's not Autumn Hayes' murder. I don't know whose corpse Doc Turner has downtown, but it ain't Autumn Hayes."

Jesse Phillips' face was ashen. Matt and Ignatius gawked at Ben expectantly.

"I first became suspicious when I examined the body again," Ben went on. "I noticed that the corpse had a suntan, like women can get at beauty salons. The tan covered practically her whole body. That was the problem. It covered her too well. When I examined the left hand of the victim, her ring finger was perfectly tanned. There was no white circle indicating that she had not worn a wedding band. And Autumn Hayes was married."

Ignatius grunted. "If that's all you got to go on, Ben, I think it's pretty weak. She could have just chosen to take the ring off before tanning."

"I ain't through yet. I found something else while examining her hands. On the middle finger of her right hand there was a little lump. Doc said it was sorta like a callus. He says that that kind of lump is often on the middle finger of a person's writing hand."

"So?" prompted Matt.

"So, Autumn Hayes was left handed. Caryn Shipley told you that Autumn Hayes claimed that left-handed people were more creative lovers, and boasted that she was left handed. Well, I say our victim is right handed.

"Also, examination of the body showed no proof that she'd had sex recently. Well, we know that John Jeffreys had been with her the day before she died. Now, I'm on shaky ground with this one, I admit. Doc says other things could prevent that from showing up, but it still raised a red flag.

Ben cleared his throat. "Then I examined the clothes that the victim had been wearing. She had been wearing gloves. The fingers of the right-hand glove were considerably more worn than the fingers of the left-hand glove, once again suggesting that the victim was right handed.

"Next, I inspected her shoes. She had been wearing a pair of heavy, high heel, black boots. The side of the right boot was badly scuffed. Now I have the same problem with the side of my right boot. It comes from driving so much. When I press the accelerator, I turn my right foot slightly on its side. Pretty soon, my boot is scuffed in the same way as the victim's boot was. Caryn Shipley told you that when Autumn came to work at Computech, she didn't drive. I checked with some of her friends here in Winchester, and they agree--Autumn did not drive an automobile.

"So, gentlemen," Ben said, "what's your take so far?"

The men remained silent as they absorbed the information that Ben had disclosed.

"Ben, I see one big hole here," Ignatius said "You forget that you have a positive identification of the body. Matt here has known the woman for almost a year. He's seen her numerous times about the neighborhood. He identified the victim as Autumn Hayes."

"I thought about that, too, 'Natius. Matt was forced to view a body in Autumn Hayes' backyard. It was the body of a tall, dark-haired girl. Her head was bashed in and her face covered with blood. He didn't look any longer than he had to, which is completely understandable. Under the circumstances, he concluded that the victim was Autumn

Hayes." Ignatius looked to Matt for confirmation. "Matthew?"

"Well, I certainly can't dispute the possibility of a mistaken identity. I had no desire to inspect the body closely. That was my first encounter with such a grisly mess. I remember wanting to vomit."

"Yeah...sorry to put you through that, Matthew," Ben said sympathetically.

"It still seems circumstantial," Ignatius protested.

"Any one piece of the circumstantial evidence in itself wouldn't be adequate. But all together...if it looks like a fish and smells like a fish, I call it a fish. Besides, I don't think it's gonna be that hard to get a positive identification on the body eventually."

Ever the cynic, Ignatius spoke up, "Well, Ben, if the body you've got down there isn't Autumn Hayes...who is she?"

"I don't like to guess--"

"No, we don't want any conjecture here," Ignatius interrupted derisively.

Ben ignored the sarcasm. "I don't like to guess, but I would bet that it's Spring Reynolds. Brian Axelrod said they were practically look-alikes when they were little girls. As women...who knows how much they still resembled each other?

"I think Spring was visiting her sister. She went out to fetch logs before the storm got worse. The murderer mistook her for Autumn. She's struck hard. Down and out. Then you see the body and call 911. Matt arrives on the scene shortly after we do. Under the gruesome circumstances, he mistakenly identifies the body as that of his neighbor, Autumn Hayes. Since her husband died in the blizzard, the one person who could certainly identify her is dead. So we conduct an investigation assuming that the victim is Autumn Hayes."

It was Matt's turn to test Ben's theory. "If the body you have is not Autumn Hayes, then where is she?"

"Good question, Matthew. When I left the office tonight, I had a notion that Autumn was the murderer and Spring the victim. Figured it was some kind of family thing. However, with Matthew's discovery that Hope Henley Dixson was Ida Phillips' niece, I no longer think Autumn killed her sister," said Ben, turning to face Jesse Phillips. "And that is where you come in, Mr. Phillips. Where is Autumn Hayes?"

Jesse Phillips looked at Ben, astounded. "Me? Why ask me, Sheriff? Hey, I got my hands full taking care of Ida. You certainly don't think that I'd be carrying on with some woman, do you? Hell, I'm so tired at night that I can hardly drag myself to bed."

Ben stepped closer to Jesse and looked at him squarely. "Mr. Phillips, when I came up here tonight, I knew that we had been mistaken in our identification of the victim. I knew she was most likely Spring. I knew that Autumn Hayes might still be alive. And I knew that if she is alive that we had to find her as soon as possible. What I didn't know was where I was gonna start looking.

"When we got here and discovered the ruckus that was going on, I got suspicious. When Matt told me that Hope Henley Dixson might be your wife's niece, I put two and two together. Now I know where I'm gonna start looking for Autumn Hayes, Mr. Phillips. At your house."

Ben made a gesture and a move toward the door. "Let's go."

Jesse Phillips did not move. He looked frozen, frantic. "Sheriff, you've got it all wrong. Okay...okay...Hope Dixson was Ida's niece. But Ida never knew about Autumn. I swear."

"It won't work, Mr. Phillips. How do you explain the dog?"

"She was confused. She just saw a white dog and thought it was Baby. She reacts that way to every dog that resembles Baby."

Suddenly, Pete raised his head and barked.

"And how do you explain that, Mr. Phillips. Pete responded to the name Baby. And he certainly appeared to recognize your wife."

Jesse Phillips' face took on a sullen, angry look. "WHY?" he wailed, shaking his fist and rolling his eyes heavenward, "Why on earth did that devil move to this town? If I'd known who she was, I'd never have sold that lot to her husband, Jim Hayes. Hayes looked me up at work one day. Said he and his wife were friends of Joe Dixson back at Computech. He said Joe told them that I had lakeside property for sale. Oh, Lord, I never dreamed that he was married to Autumn Reynolds! I sold him the property. When I first saw her, over in the yard, I thought...it can't be. I'd seen her at Hope's funeral. She was crying and carrying on. But she still had time to comfort Hope's husband, Joe. People talked a lot that day, and it got back to Ida. Things were bad enough with the suicide and all, but to think that her precious Hope had suffered because of that devil was too much for her to bear. Then, to top it off, we realized that Joe gave Baby to Autumn. She ain't been right since."

"Mr. Phillips, was that you at the Hayes house the night after the murder?" Matt asked.

"Yes, I went over there looking for Baby. I thought having the dog might calm Ida down."

"Then it was your light I saw through the windows."

"Yeah. I just used a pen flashlight. Didn't want to attract any attention. Sorry I scared you, Matt."

There was a long silence. Finally, Jesse Phillips continued. "I think I knew from the day she moved in here that there would be tragedy. Guess I'm surprised it took this long for things to come to a head. I'm just real sorry about that young girl laying up there at the morgue. Lord knows I would have done anything to keep another young woman from suffering because of that she-devil."

Ben interrupted Jesse's narration. "Mr. Phillips, please tell us what happened that morning."

"Well, it ain't really much to tell," he stated simply. "We knew we was supposed to get an even bigger storm that day. Ida always gets real nervous when the weather gets bad. She kept going to the window and looking out. I was real busy wrapping the pipes in the laundry room 'cause they froze the last time we had a big freeze. Then all of a sudden, Ida appears at the door of the laundry room. She was spattered all over with blood...I mean really covered...her hands, her dress, even her shoes. I screamed, 'Ida, what have you done?' She just looked at me real peaceful like and said, 'Jess, she won't hurt nobody else'. Then she went into the living room and put on that song she always plays, Whispering Hope, and sat down to rocking.

"I went flying over to the Hayes yard. I knew something terrible had happened. I wasn't prepared for what I saw, though. I remember standing over the body. I thought it was Autumn Hayes. I was trying to think of what to do. I couldn't have been there more than a few minutes, but it seemed like an eternity. Then I heard a scream. I turned to see this woman tearing down the yard. She was ranting and raving. When she got close enough for me to get a good look, I almost fainted. I thought the devil had come back to life. It was Autumn Hayes. She jumped on me and knocked me down. She was one strong sister. Don't ask me how, but I got in one good punch. She fell to the ground. Out like a light."

Ben cleared his throat, and in a hoarse voice said, "Mr. Phillips, where is Autumn Hayes now?"

The old man sighed. "I didn't know what to do with her. I couldn't just let her go. It's Ida, Sheriff. She'd have Ida arrested. I couldn't let Ida be arrested for this. She's so pitiful. She needs special care. I don't know what would happen to her in jail. She gets so frightened...like a little child."

Ben reached over and patted his arm. "I understand, Mr. Phillips. So what did you do with Autumn Hayes?"

"I put her in a real safe place. You know where it is, don't you, Matt? Ain't it a real safe place?"

CHAPTER 25

All eyes turned to stare at Matt. Matt's jaw dropped, and he stammered, "Who ...me? How...how would I know if she's in a safe place?"

"Matt, I told you before. I told you about my safe place where you could come in an emergency. You and your family were always welcome to take shelter there if you needed to." Jesse Phillips' cautious response revealed his reluctance to disclose the whereabouts of Autumn Hayes.

Matt stared at Jesse for what seemed to be an eternity. Suddenly his confused look changed to understanding. He jumped to his feet. "Oh no! Come on, Ben. Quick!" Matt was pulling on his coat and heading for the door.

Matt ran across the snowy lawn. The snow was covered with a frozen crust of ice. He slipped several times, but quickly regained his footing. He was aware of footsteps and voices behind him. Expletives traveled through the bitter cold air. The luminous orange moon provided light that guided them through the night. Matt sped pass the Jeffreys' place. The house showed no sign of life. He clamored up the hill where the Phillips' house faced the scene of the brutal murder. He paused, his eyes darting from one house to the other. Behind him, footsteps continued to advance, and soon Ben and Dexter were beside Matt.

"Matthew," Ben wheezed breathlessly, "what's going on? What's Phillips jabbering about?"

"This way, I think," Matt might have been talking to himself. "I think back here.--"

"Matthew..." Ben shouted after him.

Matt charged into the Phillips' yard where he thought the driveway should be. He soon realized that he had missed the spot. His foot plunged into the ditch and Matt went down. Ben and Dexter were at his side.

"Matt, you okay?" sputtered Ben.

The pain in Matt's foot told him that he was not "okay". With Ben and Dexter's help, he managed to struggle to his feet. Antonio and Scott heard the commotion from inside the Phillips' house. The front door to the house flew open.

"Who's there? Sheriff, is that you? What's going on?"

"It's all right, Antonio," answered Ben. "Just take care of Ida Phillips. We're okay out here."

Matt was in excruciating pain. He wondered if his foot were broken. "Ben, help me. We've got to get to the back of the house."

As Ben and Dexter provided support, Matt directed the men to the woods beyond the back of the house. Snow-covered underbrush gave the appearance of soft pillows scattered about the woods. They had not gone far before their path was obstructed by a curious object. It resembled a snow-covered periscope protruding from the ground.

"What the...Matt, what is that?" asked Ben.

Matt did not take the time to answer Ben's question. "Quick...this way, I think."

Matt hobbled to the right and headed in the direction of what appeared to be a small, snow-covered hill. He used his gloved hand to remove the snow on the "hillside". His companions watched in amazement as Matt uncovered, not earth, but part of a concrete structure. Frantically, Ben and Dexter began to help Matt brush away the snow. Soon a metal door appeared. Activity ceased as the three men stared dumbfounded at a metal bar that prevented the door from being opened from the inside.

"Good Lord, Sheriff," squeaked Dexter, "what in the world is this place?"

"This is a fallout shelter. The heavy door was supposed to keep people out, not in," Matt said as he removed the bar from its brackets and tossed it aside. Snow had drifted against the entrance to the shelter, hindering efforts to open the door. Once again, the men used their hands to scrape away the snow. As they pulled open the heavy door, they were struck by a sharp odor. It was the smell of mildew and rot. Dexter stepped forward and pointed the flashlight downward. Its beam illuminated steep, narrow concrete steps that disappeared into the darkness. Matt was struck with fear as he stared at the portentous black stairwell that he had dreamed about.

"I'll go first," said Ben, taking the flashlight from Dexter. "Watch your step, now."

The stairway was wet and treacherous, and Matt's foot throbbed with each step. As they descended, the men were engulfed in silence. It was as if they had descended into an abyss where no sound existed. Each step took them deeper and deeper.

It was Ben who spoke first. "You two okay?"

"Okay," reported Dexter.

"Not too good, Ben," complained Matt. "I think I broke my ankle or something--"

"Shhhh," whispered Ben.

They had reached a place where the stairwell made an abrupt turn in its decent. As the men crept around the bend, the smell of burning kerosene permeated their nostrils. A faint glow could be seen in the distance. The glow was from a portable kerosene heater. It was like a night light that might be placed in a frightened child's room. From the center of the glow floated a chilling sound. A soft voice sang hauntingly. The words were almost indiscernible. The men moved closer, careful not to make a sound. Then the mournful voice, a child's voice, sang slowly...softly.

"Put your arms around me, honey, hold me tight... Huddle up and cuddle up with all your might... Um, um won't you roll those eyes..."

The men stepped into a circle of light that was generated by the kerosene heater. The chanting ceased abruptly. After a few moments, a child-like voice said, "Is that you, Grand? Can we come out now, Grand? I'll be good. I promise I'll be good. Grand...please..." The voice broke off into sobs.

On an old army cot, stained with mildew, a pathetic form huddled against a pillow. A brown blanket concealed most of the face. Frightened brown eyes peered above the cover, and a little voice again pled, "Please, Grand...can we come out now? I'm sorry...I'm sorry..." The plea was followed by timorous crying.

Matt crept forward and gently pulled away the blanket. Autumn Hayes' hair was a mass of tangles, and her cheek displayed a red and blue bruise. She wore a dingy pink sweatsuit and heavy gym socks caked with mud. As the men gawked in disbelief, she closed her eyes tightly and shrunk away from Matt.

Scampering to the other end of the bed, she huddled in a corner, "Please, Grand, I'll be good...I'll be good..." She crumpled onto the cot again. Soon, the dark corners of her cell were filled with sobs of the child who had been Autumn Hayes.

It took the rescue squad more than an hour to move Autumn Hayes from the underground prison to the ambulance at the bottom of the hill.

When she was safely inside, Ben said, "Take it easy now, boys."

"Sure thing, Sheriff. We'll give her a slow and easy ride to the hospital. And don't worry...that other ambulance will be here before you know it. We're real busy, and we gotta move slow in this snow."

"Well, no need for that ambulance to be rushing out here. We got everything under control for the time being."

The door slammed closed, and the ambulance drove slowly down the hill. Ben turned to Matt, who was leaning against the patrol car. "Matthew, I still think you should have gone on in to the hospital to have that foot checked."

"Not on your life. After all I've put into this I intend to see this thing played out." He grabbed the arm that Ben extended, and the two men hiked back toward Ignatius' house.

They were greeted at the door by Pete, who sniffed them and rushed back to report to Ignatius. "Come on back here, you two. It's about time. You've been gone for nigh on two hours. An ambulance struggles up the hill. People rush about, carrying somebody on a stretcher...what the hell's going on? Matt, you okay?"

With Ben's assistance, Matt made it to the sofa and collapsed. Ben knelt down and removed Matt's boot. The ankle and foot were swollen.

"Think I broke my damned ankle, Nate," groaned Matt.

Suddenly Ben's attention turned from Matt's injury to the empty rocking chair. His eyes quickly searched the room. He raced to the kitchen, then the bathroom.

"Where's Jesse Phillips?" Ben demanded.

Ignatius gasped. "Why, he left when you did. I assumed that he followed you...wherever you went. You didn't expect me to restrain him, did you?" Ignatius glared at Ben.

"Oh, no...!" Ben hurried for the door. Matt stood up as if to follow.

Ben turned abruptly. "Now, you stay off that foot, damn it!"

The door banged shut, and Ben was gone. Matt dropped onto the sofa, his foot throbbing.

"Well, are you gonna' tell me or what?" snapped Ignatius.

The front door of the Phillips' house burst open and Ben raced in. Scott, Neil, and Antonio leaped from their chairs, hands beside their firearms.

"Sheriff, is something wrong?"

Ben tore down the hall. He flung open the door to what he assumed to be the bedroom. Then he stopped abruptly and stared at the pathetic scene before him. Laying on the bed in a fetal position was Ida Phillips. Clutched in her arms was a small stuffed white poodle with a red nose and black plastic eyes. Seated on the bed beside her was Jesse Phillips. His elbows were propped on his knees, and his face was buried in his hands. His shoulders jerked spastically as he sobbed. Ben leaned against the door frame and dropped his head ruefully.

CHAPTER 26

A dazzling sun sparkled in the winter sky. Rooftops appeared as snow melted and dripped into shimmering icicles that hung precariously from the eaves of houses. Patches of white were scattered about on the red muddy ground. Wild birds twittered and fought over the freshly filled bird feeders. Cars, still splattered with muddy salt water, moved freely up and down the hill. Telephones rang, televisions blared, and fallen limbs were cut into firewood. The biggest blizzard to hit the South this century finally moved in a northeasterly direction and eventually died at sea.

Matt, Ben, and Ignatius relaxed before the Sunday afternoon basketball game between Duke and North Carolina State. Tensions of the past few days eased as Ignatius served his special chili, homemade bread, and an assortment of cheeses. Matt's foot was in a cast, and he propped it up on a stool. Ben gazed pensively into the fire. Ignatius reached for his pipe. It had to happen. The conversation turned to what was now referred to as the Spring Reynolds murder.

"You know what amazes me?" Ben said. "It's the damnedest coincidence that Jim Hayes and his new bride moved to Winchester, of all places. Of all the towns and all the cities in the country, he moved to Winchester...and right across the street from Hope Dixson's aunt."

"I've thought about that, too," said Matt. "But it's not too strange that he'd come to work at the Center. Jim Hayes worked in a highly specialized area of research. And if he wanted to stay in the Southeast there's not that many places for him to get a job. I can easily see him ending up at the Center. But as for living across the street from Ida Phillips, yes, that is quite a coincidence."

"Knowing what we do about Autumn Hayes, she probably put Jim Hayes up to buying property across the street from Hope's aunt. Autumn probably got some sick kick out of tormenting the poor soul. She must have known Ida would recognize her. Well, more extraordinary things have happened," said Ignatius, puffing smoke from his pipe.

"Here's something I don't understand," continued Matt. "Why do you suppose Jesse Phillips volunteered the information that Autumn and Jim Hayes had worked at Computech? He must have known you would follow up on that lead."

"He knew I'd find out from Personnel out at the Center anyway. He also knew you'd worked there. He thought it would draw suspicion away from him if he appeared to be helping out," explained Ben. "One thing that I'm mighty pleased about is that I never took a formal statement from the Jeffreys family. Far as I'm concerned, I never heard any of that stuff about John and Sean messing around with Autumn Hayes. Phillips gave a complete statement, and I don't see why that boy has to suffer anymore."

"I feel the same way," said Matt, thinking of Chad and Garth. "I keep thinking about that pitiful child we found in that fallout shelter. I cringe to think of what those two little girls went through while they were living with Grand. It's understandable how a person could be traumatized for life. Yet, you hear of other children who experience similar abuse, and they go on to live normal, productive lives. Many victims go on to help other people who suffered the same kind of abuse they experienced. What determines the difference?"

Ignatius grunted. "There's no rational explanation for irrational behavior. Autumn Hayes and Ida Phillips *acted* irrationally. Jesse Phillips *REacted* irrationally. You can't keep going back and going back over the same old stuff...you have to deal with what's up today." Ignatius puffed heartily on his pipe, generating clouds of smoke. He appeared to be pleased with his explanation.

"I don't know, Nate. Seems like such a waste. Autumn Hayes was apparently very intelligent," Matt added.

"So was Ted Bundy," Ignatius replied. "People who are sociopaths often have high IQ's. And if you ask me that's what Autumn Hayes was...a dag-gone sociopath. Frankly, I'm glad that whole thing is over. I kept feeling like I was peeping in my neighbors' windows. I don't like knowing all this stuff about other people's business."

"Well, I'm just glad my part in this is over," Ben announced. "We checked with American Airlines at Nashville International Airport. On the Sunday night preceding the murder, a young woman claimed a reservation made for one Spring Reynolds on the 6 p.m.

flight from Orlando, Florida to Nashville, Tennessee. According to a friend, who had made the business trip with Jim Hayes, Hayes complained of being exhausted because he'd made a trip to the Nashville airport the night before. Hayes and Autumn met Spring on Sunday night. Then he drove Autumn and Spring back to Winchester, and the next morning he drove all the way back to Nashville to catch the plane to Buffalo."

There was a long silence as the Matt and Ignatius sorted the new information Ben reported.

Finally Matt lifted his leg from the stool and sat upright. "If Spring arrived on Sunday night before the murder, where do you suppose she was when John and Sean Jeffreys paid their visits to Autumn?"

"I've given that a lot of thought myself, Matthew. Most likely she was right there in the house," Ben said. Matt affected a look of disgust.

"Yeah, seems sick that Autumn would carry on like that with her own sister in the house. But that's what seems to have happened," said Ben.

"SICK!!! My granny's eyeball!!!" bellowed Ignatius. "That's not sick. That's evil. The woman was just what Phillips said. She was a devil, and Spring too. Why I wouldn't be surprised if Spring had her eye to the keyhole. Remember John Jeffreys said Autumn smiled wickedly when she stood naked on the steps. Mark my word...she was smiling for Spring's benefit."

Ignatius lifted his pipe and began to puff huge clouds of smoke in the air. Pete, realized Ignatius was distressed. He stood, barked sharply three times, circled his bed, and then lay back down.

"Hey Nate," said Matt. "Who's conjecturing now?"

"Matt's right, 'Natius," said Ben. "We've got to face the fact that there're some loose ends that'll never be tied up. Sometimes we just have to let things go and settle for what we know is absolute proof.

"We have proof that the body we had at the morgue is Spring Reynolds. She was positively identified as Spring Reynolds by fingerprints from Florida Corrections. Seems like Spring had a brush with the law down there. Since we couldn't find Spring's next of kin, Grady Hayes offered to take care of the arrangements for her.

"He's taking care of Autumn, too. Technically, Autumn broke no laws. Hayes has moved her to a private sanitarium out in Texas. She was still senseless when she left the hospital here. Thought she was a little girl."

Ben paused, sighed and then continued, "Poor man. Never met a nicer fella. Buried his son, his son's sister-in-law, and now he's footing the bill for Autumn's treatment.

"As for Jesse Phillips...that was kidnapping pure and simple when he locked up Autumn Hayes. DA still let him out on bond on account of Ida but the man's not going anywhere. I don't think Ida will ever stand trial for murder. She's up in Nashville now undergoing psychiatric testing. How in the world do you go about testing someone like that?"

No one answered.

The trees created shadows against the setting sun. The fire burned low, and Matt began to nod in reaction to his pain medication. Pete arose and stretched. Then, spying his new master, he trotted across the room and jumped on Ignatius' lap. Ignatius scratched the dog's ear affectionately.

Ben broke the silence. "You know...I feel awfully relieved about this case being solved. But one thing has puzzled me for days. I just can't rest till I figure it out."

"Just *one* thing? What is it?" asked Matt, roused again from his nap.

"Well, going back to that very first day when we found the body of Spring Reynolds, I've felt that you two have been holding back on me..."

Both Matt and Ignatius opened their mouths to protest. Ben held up a palm to them.

"No. Now the murder has been solved. Without a doubt, Mrs. Phillips committed the murder. So even if you are withholding information, it's not interfering with the prosecution but I must admit, I am curious. It's like having this big jigsaw puzzle with a piece missing. I feel like I'll never see the complete picture."

Matt and Ignatius looked at each other. They could tell that their friend was hurt. Finally Ignatius spoke. "Tell him, Matt. There's no reason not to. The investigation is over."

Ben looked at Matt expectantly. Matt told him about the dream in which he watched the murder of Spring Reynolds. He told him of how he had shared the dream with Ignatius, and how they decided that the dream might detract from rather than help with the investigation. He confided in Ben that there were other instances in which his dreams had become reality. He related the scene from Jill's funeral, and the dream of Garth being lost in Walmart. Matt also described the nightmares that had tormented him throughout the investigation.

"So, you see, Ben," said Matt, "we weren't withholding evidence. Quite the contrary, my dreams could never be used as evidence in a court of law. We just felt that the information might sidetrack you, make you miss something important."

Ben's face lit up, "Is that all it was? Shh...it! Why, y'all oughta told me. It's a gift! Lots of folks have dreams to warn them or prepare them for something 'bout to happen." Matt and Ben smiled. "That's right. Some folks say it's just mojo. I say it's a gift. My Mama was like that, Matt. She was all times having dreams come true. I wouldn't have thought nothing of it if you'd told me. I'm used to that."

"Well, I should have known you would be," Matt mused.

The three men laughed.

Ben drove Matt up the hill to his house and accompanied him as he hobbled through the mud to his front door. "Want to come in, Ben?"

"No Matthew gotta get on back. Sure you're okay?"

Assuring Ben that he would be okay, Matt entered the house to be greeted by the feline duo. Wary of the crutches their friend wielded, the cats soon scampered back to the safety of higher ground. Spencer jumped up on the kitchen counter, while Aslan peered down from atop the refrigerator.

"Not time to eat yet," declared Matt, and he limped down the hall toward his study. He dropped into the recliner and elevated his throbbing foot. Matt wanted to be comforted, stroked, and listened to. He reached for the phone and dialed Caryn's number.

"Hello...," that soft, enticing voice whispered in his ear.

"Caryn? Matt."

"Oh Matt. And how is the foot today?"

"Hurts like hell. I need somebody to take care of me, stroke me, to fetch things for me."

"Sounds to me like you need a dog, Matt." A bit of contempt was evident in her voice.

"Sorry...let me start again. Hello, Caryn. I need someone to help me, to hold me, and to listen to me. Better?"

"Much better."

"Caryn, you know what I've been thinking about during this whole damned blizzard?"

"No."

"I've been thinking that maybe I need to go to the Outer Banks...you know, climb Jockey Ridge, hang glide off the dunes, bicycle down the beach, wind surf...and might even go down to Hatteras and do a little surfing. Who knows?"

"Ah, yes, who knows?"

"And Caryn know what else would be nice?"

"What, Matt?"

"It would be nice if you were there."

There was a long pause.

"Matt, when do you plan this sentimental journey?"

"Oh, I don't know...soon."
"Well let me know when you decide. Okay?"
"Okay, Caryn."
"Take care, Matt. Take real good care."

The End

Made in the USA
Charleston, SC
28 November 2016